Wild THING
GETS A DOG!

Look out for

Wild THING

Wild THING
GETS A DOG!

Emma Barnes

Illustrated by Jamie Littler

SCHOLASTIC

First published in the UK in 2014 by Scholastic Children's Books
An imprint of Scholastic Ltd
Euston House, 24 Eversholt Street
London, NW1 1DB, UK
Registered office: Westfield Road, Southam, Warwickshire, CV47 0RA
SCHOLASTIC and associated logos are trademarks and/
or registered trademarks of Scholastic Inc.

ISBN 978 1407 13796 4

A CIP catalogue record for this book is
available from the British Library.

Printed and bound by CPI Group (UK) Ltd, Croydon, CR0 4YY
Papers used by Scholastic Children's Books are made
from wood grown in sustainable forests.

1 3 5 7 9 10 8 6 4 2

This is a work of fiction. Names, characters, places,
incidents and dialogues are products of the author's imagination
or are used fictitiously. Any resemblance to actual people,
living or dead, events or locales is entirely coincidental.

www.scholastic.co.uk

To Abby and her hound

Wild THING

She's a demon child
She's not meek and mild
She's wild!
Oh yeah. . .

She can bite
Oh yeah and she can fight!
She'll give you a fright!
Oh yeah!

She's wild, wild, wild!
Yeah!
Oh she's wild, wild, wild. . .

It was just an ordinary Thursday.

I was doing my homework at the kitchen table, Dad was searching the fridge for something for tea, and my little sister, Wild Thing, was under the table "cooking" something in her toy kitchen. She makes all kinds of horrible things in it, but so far nobody's ever had to eat any of it, thank goodness, because all the food is plastic. (Mind you, I think Wild Thing has tried, because some of the hot dogs and cupcakes have teeth marks.)

"I was sure we had some leftover rice. . ." Dad muttered. "And some tomatoes."

"Stir it round, stir it round!" chortled Wild Thing. She was bent over the mixing bowl with her long hair dangling down and an evil expression on her face, like a witch stirring her cauldron.

"We even seem to have run out of tuna," said Dad, peering into the cupboard. "I was sure there was one more tin."

"Don't want tuna," said Wild Thing, and she cackled an evil cackle.

"There aren't any baked beans, either."

Wild Thing cackled again and suddenly I got suspicious.

"Wait a minute. What have you got in that bowl?"

Wild Thing said nothing.

"The tuna's in there, isn't it? And the rice?"

Wild Thing still said nothing, but put her arms protectively round the mixing bowl.

"Josephine!" said Dad in his special stern voice. Josephine is Wild Thing's real name.

"It's for my lovely stew!" shouted Wild Thing. "Nobody said I couldn't!"

"Nobody said I couldn't" is one of my sister's favourite defences whenever she's in trouble.

"Nobody said I couldn't cut Kate's homework into

a hundred pieces."

"Nobody said I couldn't glue a napkin to my nose."

"Nobody said I couldn't pour tomato ketchup over my head when I'm playing vampires."

"Nobody said I couldn't pretend Dad's guitar case was a canoe and paddle it down the stairs."

"I'm glad your stew is so lovely," said Dad sternly, "because that's what YOU are going to have for dinner."

"No!" squawked Wild Thing. "Won't!"

But for once, Dad seemed cross enough to make her do it. I watched, fascinated, as he got a big spoon out of the kitchen drawer and marched over to her mixing bowl. Then he spooned up a dollop and held it out to Wild Thing, while my sister put her hand over her mouth, screeching as loud as she could.

"Here. You made it, so you can eat it—" Dad stopped short, staring at the gloopy mixture on the spoon. "Wait. Why is this stuff green?"

He was right. The lumps of tuna and rice and baked beans (and I thought I could spot pineapple chunks too) were all floating around in a bright green gloop.

"What's she put in there?" I wondered. "Frozen spinach? Lime cordial? Mint ice cream?"

"Not telling," said Wild Thing.

My dad dipped a finger into the mixture, then stuck it into his mouth. He almost fell over. "Yeurrrgh! That's disgusting!"

It was at that moment that I spotted the empty plastic bottle on the floor. "Pine Fresh Washing-up Liquid," I read aloud. "She's used the whole bottle."

However cross he was, Dad wasn't about to feed Wild Thing washing-up-liquid stew. "That still leaves the question of what we have for dinner," he said, as he dumped her mixing bowl in the sink.

"Takeaway?" I suggested hopefully.

"We did that yesterday. We can't keep doing it."

"Lucky Dip!" cried Wild Thing.

We all looked at each other. Dad hesitated. I was sure he was going to be all sensible and say no.

"Oh, go on then," he said.

We all went into the back hall, where we keep the washing machine, the hiking boots, the sled and lots of things that we don't use that often. There's also our freezer. It's one of those big old-fashioned freezers, like a huge trunk you open from the top.

"It's a bit empty," I said, peering in. "Most of the stuff's right at the bottom."

Dad was tying a scarf over my sister's eyes. He stepped back and looked at her. "Are you sure about this?"

"Want to do Lucky Dip!" Wild Thing howled.

So Dad grabbed Wild Thing's middle. Then he dangled her over the freezer by her ankles.

Or rather, that's what he tried to do. I guess she'd been growing lately. Or maybe it was because all the food was at the very bottom of the freezer. Anyway, there was a lot of

heaving, swinging and shouting from Wild
Thing, while Dad tried to hold her upside
down by one leg, and I helpfully grabbed hold
of the other.

"Keep hold. . ."

"I *am* keeping hold. . ."

"Stop wriggling, Wild Thing!"

"But I can't reach!" Wild Thing screeched. She wriggled harder, trying to grab the packets of frozen food, and Dad pulled, and I pushed, and then – *CRASH!* – suddenly Wild Thing went slipping out of our grasp, right into the freezer. We were all so surprised that for a moment we didn't say anything. Dad and me just gasped like a pair of goldfish, while Wild Thing sat at the bottom of the freezer with oven chips in her hair.

Then we all began to laugh.

Suddenly there was a cough from behind us. Gran was standing in the doorway.

"Is there some reason why you have put poor Josephine in the freezer?" she asked. Her voice was as icy as the chips.

2

Even when Gran understood what we'd been doing, she didn't approve. We were back in the kitchen, and Gran was standing in the middle of the floor, hands on hips, glaring.

"So let me get this straight. When you couldn't decide what to cook, you used to take Josephine, blindfold her, bob her into the freezer and whatever she pulled out, that was what you ate?"

"Got it in one," said Dad, a bit defiantly.

"Wild Thing got the idea from the Lucky Dip at the school fair," I said.

Wild Thing wasn't paying attention. She was too busy winding her hair round the frozen chips as if they were curlers. Then she experimentally moved one chip towards her nostril – until Gran barked, "Josephine!" and she quickly dropped it again.

Gran turned back to Dad.

"So what happened if she pulled out lollies and chicken stock? Is that what you'd eat?"

"That's what we'd eat."

"That's the whole point," I explained. "You never knew what you'd get."

"It was fun!" Wild Thing agreed.

Gran tutted. "It's not what *I'd* call a balanced meal."

I love Gran. But there's no doubt she can be a bit of an old granpuss sometimes. We've had some great meals from Lucky Dip. Pizza with chocolate sauce. Potato waffles with ice cubes. Strawberries with hot dogs. OK, they may not sound great to you. But we always ate them. And enjoyed them. Sort of.

Of course Gran didn't see it that way. Still, once she had stopped tutting, she helped Dad make a really nice meal, much nicer than if we'd had Lucky Dip. Gran managed to find some eggs Dad had overlooked, and turned them into an omelette. We had peas from the freezer, as well as potato wedges and lashings of tomato ketchup. While we were eating, the doorbell rang.

It was Wes, the lead singer in Dad's old rock band, Monkey Magic. Dad doesn't play with them much any more. But he's still good friends with them, and he often writes songs for the band.

Gran doesn't really approve of Monkey Magic (or rock music) but she does have a bit of a soft spot for Wes. He always remembers to ask how her tango classes are going. And he always praises her cooking. "This omelette is magnificent," he said. "I've eaten omelettes all over the world but you can't beat this."

Gran preened herself. Then she said she had to get home, because she had a big work meeting next day. Wes told her he wouldn't see her for a while, because the band was off to the USA.

"New York, Austin, Denver, San Francisco," said Wes dreamily. "Our first big American tour."

"Wow!" I said. And while Dad and Wes lounged in the living room, strumming their guitars, Wild Thing and I bombarded Wes with questions.

"Yeah – it's going to be great," Wes said. "Hey, you should come with us, man," he said suddenly to Dad. "Back on the road again! You know you want to."

Dad shook his head.

"But you should be there, Tom. After all, you wrote half the songs."

"My touring days are over," said Dad, trying out a new riff.

"Why, man?"

"You know why. Because of the girls."

"Bring them along!" said Wes, waving a hand at Wild Thing and me, and nearly knocking over his coffee.

Wild Thing and me looked at each other.

"Yeah, we'll come too!" Wild Thing urged.

"I'd love to go to America!" I said.

"There's that small thing called school," said Dad.

"They can miss it," said Wes.

"Yeah, we can miss it," Wild Thing said. I nodded. Time off school to go touring the US of A with Monkey Magic? You bet I wanted to go.

"Absolutely not," said Dad firmly. "The girls need to go to school. Their education is important. Besides," he added to Wes, "you've got Chris now. You don't need two guitarists."

Wes gave a big sigh. Wild Thing and I sighed too. For a moment we had dreamed that we might really get to go. But we should have known Dad would never let us.

You see, ever since our mum died, it's been down to Dad to bring us up, and he takes his responsibilities seriously. He says family life and playing in a rock band don't mix. He still plays the guitar, but he spends most of his time teaching or song-writing or working in his studio. He never goes on tour any more, even though we'd love to go with him. I can just imagine it now – sitting in the tour bus and watching the scenery roll by, waving to the fans, sitting backstage playing computer games, eating loads of junk food or else ordering room service in a fancy hotel. Dad says it isn't as much fun as it sounds – but how do we know, if he won't even let us try?

And this time it was America!

"Disneyland," I murmured. "The Grand Canyon. Hollywood."

"Zebras," said Wild Thing. "Antelopes."

I guess Wild Thing was a bit confused with her geography (after all, she is only five) because I don't think zebras and antelopes live in the USA. I didn't say anything though. I wasn't a hundred per cent sure myself.

Wes played a few mournful chords on his guitar. Then he said, "Hey, Tom, if you're sure you can't come, how about you and the girls look after Hound Dog for me? You'd like that, wouldn't you, girls?"

"Who's Hound Dog?" I asked.

"You never met Hound Dog? I got him from the Dogs' Home. His real name's Elvis. But you see, he ain't nothing but a Hound Dog. So that's what I call him." He and Dad shared a chuckle.

Wild Thing and I looked at each other, then looked at Dad.

"Perlease, perlease, can we look after Hound Dog!" I begged.

"Yeah – want a doggy!" shrieked Wild Thing.

"Absolutely not," said Dad. "I've got a rule – two beasties are enough."

"But Goldilocks and Bug-Eyed Monster are dead," I pointed out. (Goldilocks and Bug-Eyed Monster were our goldfish.)

"I'm not talking about *pets*," said Dad.

It took me a moment to work out what he meant. Then: "*We're* not beasties!" I yelled. "C'mon, Wild Thing!"

We both flung ourselves on Dad, bashing him with cushions and jumping on him. I don't think Wild Thing had even worked out why I was cross, but she loves a rumpus, so she didn't care. As for Wes, he grabbed Dad's guitar, so it wouldn't get broken, then sat there laughing.

Dad won, eventually. He fought us off, then wrapped us up in the rug.

"The answer's still no," he panted.

"Come on, your girls are dying to have him," coaxed Wes.

"Sure they are. For five minutes. But who will end up walking him, and feeding him, and scraping his poo off the pavement?" asked Dad. "Me! That's who." He pointed at me and Wild Thing. "I had years of cleaning up THEIR poo, when they were tiny, and now I'm enjoying the rest."

And however much we begged and pleaded – "I LOVE picking up poo!" said Wild Thing – he wouldn't budge.

I could hardly believe Dad could be so hard-hearted. Then he realized the time and sent Wild Thing up to get ready for bed, and told me that I'd better get on with my homework.

After a bit Wild Thing came dancing in to kiss everyone goodnight. She was wearing her stripy tiger pyjamas, teamed up with lime-green slippers and – for some reason known only to herself – a pink shower cap that Gran uses when she stays over. I tell you, sometimes I get a headache just looking at my sister. Then she went to bed. It's not like Wild Thing to go to bed without a fuss, and I suppose I should have wondered about this. But I didn't.

"I guess I should be going too," said Wes. He slung his guitar case over his back, gave me a hug – "I'll bring you back some pressies from Stateside, Katie" – and strode out of the front door.

Or rather, that's what he tried to do.

CRASH! KERBANG! THUMP!

An avalanche of objects came hurtling down on to him. And the next moment Wes was lying motionless on the floor.

3

He's dead. That was my first thought. Stone cold dead.

My second was that it was all Wild Thing's fault. And I was right about that, for the very next moment Wild Thing appeared at the top of the stairs and started dancing about with glee.

"It worked! It worked!"

"What worked?"

"My Burglar Trap!"

"But Wes isn't a burglar!" I looked at Wes, who was lying very still, not saying anything, under a heap of Wild Thing's toys. She had balanced them over the door somehow. I reckoned she must have climbed the curtains to get up there.

Dad looked pretty worried as he leant over Wes.

"Hey, mate – wake up! Are you all right?"

Wes gave a low moan. Then he muttered something.

"What was that you said?" asked Dad, putting his ear close to Wes's mouth.

Wes began to mumble.

"Don't worry, man . . . I'll live . . . most likely . . . it's just . . . if you could just . . . if you could just . . . take my dog, man, it's all that I worry about. . . Ah, I'm seeing stars! My head!"

Dad made a growling noise – he sounded a bit like a dog himself. "All right," he grated at last. "We'll take him."

"Ah, that's terrific, man!" yelled Wes, jumping to his feet.

Dad looked at him suspiciously. "I thought you were seeing stars?"

"Yeah, yeah, I am – but it's the relief, you know, I'm recovering already." Wes rubbed his head. "Hey, what's a bit of concussion if Hound Dog's got a place to stay?"

Wild Thing went bouncing round the hall. "We're getting a doggy! We're getting a doggy!"

Dad tried to give Wild Thing a telling-off about her Burglar Trap, but of course she wouldn't listen. He groaned. "She really is completely wild," he said. "Sometimes I think it's like being the father of a – hyena."

Wild Thing didn't at all mind being compared to a hyena. She just leapt around the hall laughing like the hyenas from *The Lion King*. As for Wes, he was already out of the door. I think he wanted to make a quick getaway before Dad could change his mind.

"Oh well, I suppose one small dog can't make things any more chaotic than they are already," Dad grumbled as he started picking up Wild Thing's stuff.

"Don't you worry," I assured him. "He'll be no trouble at all."

From then on, Wild Thing and I could think of nothing except our new dog. We spent every waking moment planning for his arrival.

Here are some of the things we did:

ME

1. Got lots of library books about dogs and read them cover to cover.

2. Looked up different dog breeds on the internet.

3. Grilled my best friend, Bonnie, about her dogs, Sugar and Sweet. (Bonnie's Top Tip – don't leave your dogs alone in the same room as your birthday cake.)

4. Argued about whose bedroom the dog would sleep in (I wanted him).

WILD THING

1. Built Hound Dog a den in the hall using Dad's guitar books and music stand (Dad was not pleased).

2. Drew lots of pictures of dogs and sellotaped them to the walls to make Hound Dog feel at home (Dad was not pleased).

3. Watched the DVD of *One Hundred and One Dalmatians* seventeen times (Dad didn't mind this – until she jammed the DVD player. Then, Dad was not pleased).

4. Argued about whose bedroom the dog would sleep in (she wanted him).

"He's not sleeping in either of your bedrooms," said Dad. "In fact, he's not going to be allowed upstairs at all. I don't want dog hair everywhere. He'll sleep in his own basket in the kitchen."

Wild Thing and I weren't too happy with that. But we didn't argue. We didn't want to risk Dad changing his mind until Wes was out of the country – and it was too late.

We weren't expecting Hound Dog until Friday. On Thursday, after school, I went home with Bonnie. We were sitting in her bedroom, munching crisps and talking all things dog ("Lots of people don't realize you have to walk a dog every single day," I told Bonnie. "Yes," she agreed, "and it's very important not to feed them onions"), when my mobile rang.

I was surprised to hear Wild Thing's voice.

"Kate, come home quick!" she squeaked.

"Why? What's happened?"

"He's here!" Wild Thing shrieked. She nearly deafened me. "Elvis is here!"

Hound Dog was sitting in the middle of our kitchen. Dad and Wes drank their coffee, just as if it were any ordinary afternoon, while Wild Thing and I walked round and round Hound Dog with our mouths wide open. We couldn't believe he was here at last.

Hound Dog sat watching us with his tail wagging like crazy and his head on one side.

"He's *gorgeous!*" I said. "Gorgeous . . . and unusual." He was too. He was low down like a corgi . . . and white like a Westie . . . and he had soft, floppy ears like a collie . . . and a long, fluffy tail like a spaniel.

"What kind of dog is he?" asked Wild Thing. I was wondering the same thing.

"Hound Dog isn't really any kind of dog," said

Wes. "You see, the thing is, he's unique. There's only one dog like him in the entire world."

"You mean he's a mongrel," said Dad.

Wes looked hurt. "I mean he's unique, man."

Wild Thing asked what a mongrel was. So I explained. "It's like his mum was a Great Dane and his dad was a Dobermann and his grandma was a Chihuahua and his granddad was a pug and his other grandma and grandpa were poodles and so Elvis here ended up—"

"A mess," said Dad.

"No, very special," said Wes. "As soon as I saw him in the Dogs' Home I knew he was the dog for me." Then he patted Hound Dog on the back. "Go on, Hound Dog, say hello to Kate and Wild Thing."

Hound Dog licked our fingers. Wild Thing squealed with delight, and Hound Dog got excited and jumped up and knocked over Wes's coffee cup with his tail.

"Err, I'll bring you another from America," said Wes, putting the pieces in the bin.

"Wait a minute," said Dad. "Where's his basket?"

"What basket?"

"Well, where does he sleep? He must have a bed."

"Oh, he sleeps – he sleeps – tell you what," said Wes quickly. "I'll just nip back and get his basket."

While Wes was gone, Wild Thing showed Hound Dog the den she'd made for him. Hound Dog just looked at it. Then, when Wild Thing tried to make him go inside, he wagged his tail and knocked it over instead.

"I think he looks most like a beagle," I decided.

"He looks like a Dalmatian," said Wild Thing. (He looked nothing like a Dalmatian.)

"He looks like a mutt," said Dad.

Twenty minutes later, Wes was back. He had brought a lovely basket, which he put down in front of Hound Dog.

"In you go, boy," he said. But Hound Dog just

looked at Wes, then looked at the basket, in a puzzled sort of way.

"He looks like he doesn't know what it is," I said.

"That's a *brand new* basket," said Dad suspiciously. He looked closer. "It's still got the price tag on."

"Well, I have to go now," said Wes quickly. "Going to really miss you guys. All of you. Take care."

And he was gone.

Hound Dog didn't seem too upset. He set off to explore the house. When he got to our front room, he had a good sniff round, then jumped – PLONK – on to the sofa, where he settled himself down in the middle of the cushions.

"Hey, you're not allowed up there," said Dad. "Get down!"

Hound Dog looked at him with his head on one side.

"Down, boy!"

Hound Dog started to sit up . . .

("See," said Dad, "he can tell I mean business.")

. . . and then settled himself down again, even deeper into the softest cushions.

"Oh yeah?" I said.

So Dad marched out and fetched Hound Dog's basket, which he put on the floor in the front of him. But Hound Dog wouldn't go into his basket. Instead he rolled over on to his back and waved his legs in the air.

Wild Thing and me began to giggle.

"That's it!" Dad snapped. "I am not going to be defied by some stupid dog!" He picked up Hound Dog and dumped him in the basket.

Hound Dog jumped out of the basket. Dad positioned himself in front of the sofa and stood guarding it, with his arms and legs spread out wide, a bit like a goalkeeper in front of a goal.

Hound Dog watched him with his head on one side. Then he dodged left, dodged right, and when Dad tried to grab him, he nipped straight between Dad's legs and back on to the sofa!

Dad wiped the sweat from his forehead. Then he said, "I need a drink of water." He marched towards the door. Then he stopped and said, "What are *you* doing there?"

He was talking to Wild Thing. She was sitting in Hound Dog's basket. She just about fitted, if she scrunched up.

"I like it here," she announced. "I'm going to sit here to watch TV."

"No, you're not," said Dad. "That's the dog's basket."

"But he doesn't like it and I do."

Dad snorted and left.

I sat down on the sofa next to Hound Dog. I wondered if he would be unfriendly about me sharing it, but he wagged his tail.

"Good boy," I said.

"I like having a dog," Wild Thing announced.

"So do I," I said, stroking Hound Dog. "But I'm not sure Dad's so keen."

"Course he is!" said Wild Thing. "He loved that chasing game."

Sometimes I think Wild Thing lives on a different planet from the rest of us.

Hound Dog yawned and rolled over on to his back again. He looked really funny with his legs in the air.

"Do you think he wants his tummy tickled?" I asked.

"Try it," suggested Wild Thing.

So I tickled Hound Dog's tummy, and you could tell he enjoyed it. He wriggled a bit and made a noise like a growl, only it was a happy noise, almost like a cat purring (only, of course, Hound Dog is not a cat so it sounded different).

Wild Thing came over and tickled Hound Dog's tummy too. Then she rolled over on to her back, and lay there with her arms and legs sticking in the air. "Tickle *my* tummy, Kate!"

"You're not a dog."

"He likes it. So maybe I'll like it too."

So I tickled Wild Thing's tummy. She's very ticklish, and she began to giggle and squirm, then fell on to the floor with a crash.

"I liked that!" she announced.

I was smoothing Hound Dog's ears. They were soft and velvety.

"I think this owning a dog business is going to be a piece of cake," I said.

"Easy-peasy, lemon squeezy," said Wild Thing.

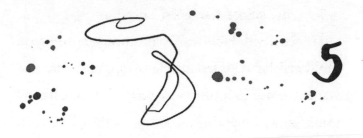

That first day we had lots of fun with Hound Dog. Though Wild Thing and I had very different ideas about what looking after dogs involved.

I tried to train him to *Sit*, *Lie down* and *Fetch*. The only one of these he was any good at was "Lie down", and I think that was because he was really tired after all the jumping about he did when I said "Sit". He did like the bits of ham I gave him for rewards, though. He always gobbled those up!

Wild Thing was more interested in dressing him up. As soon as he was snoring, she got out her black marker pen, and when I came back from fetching more ham, I found she'd inked on some big black spots. ("It's to make him look like a Dalmatian.") She also found him sunglasses, and she decorated his collar with baking foil and glitter and ribbons. Then she took a photo of him with Dad's mobile phone. (Dad was upstairs working in his studio, playing gloomy blues numbers on his guitar.)

When Hound Dog woke up, Wild Thing tried to train him to shake paws. She said he was definitely getting the idea. So far as I could see, whenever she said "Paw", all four of his paws stayed glued to the floor (though his mouth opened wide for the ham) but I decided not to argue.

Eventually Dad came downstairs.

"What have you done to him?" he groaned. He wasn't impressed with Hound Dog's spots. ("He's going to get black ink everywhere now!") He was even *less* impressed with the glitter he found stuck to his mobile phone. He was pretty grumpy as he told us to get into our coats so that we could all take Hound Dog for a walk.

When we got home, we were all starving. "We're just going to have a simple meal tonight,"

Dad announced, rummaging in the fridge. "Ham, salad and potatoes – even your gran can't say that's not a healthy, nutritious meal."

Wild Thing and I looked at each other.

"I know there was a packet of ham somewhere. . ." Dad went on.

Hound Dog gave a contented burp.

At bedtime, Wild Thing and I begged and begged Dad to let Hound Dog sleep in our rooms – we reckoned he could take turns – but Dad wasn't having any of it. Instead, Hound Dog was shut up in the kitchen with his new basket.

"If he doesn't like his basket, fine, he can sleep on the floor," said Dad. "That's up to him. But he's not, I repeat NOT, coming upstairs!"

I guess all that dog training had tired me out, because I went straight off to sleep, and didn't wake up until I dreamt I heard someone whispering in my ear. I tried to turn over. But it was no good. Someone really *was* whispering in my ear. Wild Thing!

"Wake up, Kate!" she hissed.

"What do you want?" I yawned. "What time is it anyway?" I rolled over and looked at my alarm clock. Ten past six. *Ten past six!* "Get out of my bed this moment!"

"But Kate! It's a Mergency!"

"What kind of Emergency?" I asked suspiciously. I know Wild Thing's emergencies from old. The dangerous "flood" which turns out to be Wild Thing's glass of water, which has tipped over in the night. The mountaineering accident where Wild Thing's teddy falls off the wardrobe. Even the strange case of the missing toothpaste.

"It's Hound Dog. He's vanished."

"What do you mean, vanished?"

"He's gone. Stolen! And it's *your* fault! You wouldn't let me do my Burglar Trap!"

I pushed back the covers and leapt out of bed.

She was right. The kitchen was empty – of dogs, anyway, although Hound Dog's basket was still in the middle of the floor.

I checked the front room and the hall. In fact, I checked everywhere I could think of, while Wild Thing trailed behind me, snivelling. But he wasn't on the sofa. He wasn't in the cupboard under the stairs. He wasn't in the recycling box, hiding among the tins and newspapers. He wasn't anywhere.

I turned round to see Wild Thing pressing numbers on the phone.

"What are you doing?"

"Calling the police!" she squeaked. "And the fire brigade."

"You can't do that." I lunged for the phone.

"I know the number."

"That's not the point!" I managed to wrestle the phone away from her.

"But he's been dognapped. They need to send a helicopter."

I pointed out there was no sign of a break-in. "Anyway, I don't think Hound Dog's valuable enough to steal."

"*I'd* steal him!" said Wild Thing at once.

I could just imagine it – Wild Thing in a burglar mask, with a big sack over her shoulder, climbing into somebody's house so she could grab their pet.

Personally, I was more worried that Hound Dog might have run away. After all, this was a new place, and he could've run back to his old home.

"I think we'd better wake Dad," I said.

I could hear Dad's snores from the landing. He didn't wake up when we banged on his door, and he didn't wake up when we went crashing into his room. When Wild Thing hurled herself on to his chest with a blood-curdling shriek – *then* he woke up.

"Mergency!" she screeched.

"Ermf – erruff – ooff!"

"It's important," I said. "Hound Dog's gone!"

Dad groaned. Wild Thing peered into his face and said accusingly: "You're still asleep."

"I'm *not* still asleep," said Dad. "Sad to say, I'm now one hundred per cent awake."

"No, you're not. You're still snoring!"

I opened my mouth, then stopped. Wild Thing was right. There *was* a snoring sound. But if it wasn't Dad, then who was it?

I pulled back the duvet.

"What's *he* doing there?!"

There was Hound Dog, all curled up in a round, doggy heap at the end of Dad's bed.

Wild Thing and I both turned on Dad.

"YOU SAID HE WASN'T ALLOWED UPSTAIRS!"

"I know I did – believe me, the last thing I wanted was this old furry heap sitting on my feet."

Dad explained that after Wild Thing and I had gone to bed he had sat in the front room, watching a TV show about Elvis Presley. Hound Dog watched too. ("He seemed to really enjoy it. Must be a fan.") Then Dad had gone up to bed. He had shut Hound Dog in the kitchen.

But . . . Hound Dog didn't want to be shut in the kitchen.

"I could hear him whining. Man, it went on and on! He wore me down," said Dad. "It was like somebody scraping fingernails over a blackboard. Or a tap dripping. I just couldn't take another minute."

So Dad went downstairs and opened the kitchen door. Immediately, Hound Dog streaked past him and ran straight up the stairs. Dad found Hound Dog sitting in the middle of his bed, wagging his tail. And he wouldn't budge an inch.

"I suppose I could have carried him down," said Dad pathetically. "But I couldn't face it. I was exhausted. So I let him stay. And all he's done is snore . . . and grunt . . . and every now and then he wakes up and has a good scratch . . . and then he settles himself down again, right on top of my ankles!"

Of course, Wild Thing and I were furious. We had wanted Hound Dog to sleep with *us*! But Dad said it was a one-off.

"Whatever Wes has let him get away with," he said grimly, "he's not going to rule the roost here. He's got to learn that Dogs Sleep Downstairs."

At that moment, Hound Dog woke up. He was really pleased to see us and licked our fingers, and whined and wagged his tail like anything. I think he thought it was just perfect, having the whole pack together! Wild Thing and I thought it was pretty good too, and we climbed into Dad's bed for a bit of a snuggle. I'm not sure Dad was so pleased, though. He kept groaning and complaining about our cold feet.

One thing we soon discovered about Hound Dog was that he was very laid-back about visitors. Some dogs make a big fuss about the postman, for example. Not Hound Dog. He just wagged his tail or yawned. When somebody delivered some flyers about a new pizza place, Hound Dog didn't even get up from the sofa.

"Not much of a watchdog!" said Dad.

Wild Thing took this as an insult. "You *are* a watchdog – aren't you, boy?" And she ran to the door barking fiercely, showing him what to do. But Hound Dog just looked at her and wagged his tail.

So when the doorbell rang later that afternoon, we didn't really expect any problems. I could see it was Zach and Bonnie through the glass.

I wasn't surprised as I'd already left a couple of messages for Bonnie telling her to come round and meet Hound Dog, and to bring her brother, Zach, too.

So I didn't grab hold of Hound Dog's collar. Or shut him in the kitchen. I knew he wasn't the crazy guard dog kind of dog that would leap about and make a huge fuss.

What I *couldn't* see, though, was that Zach and Bonnie's mum, Susie, was standing at the end of our path, just beyond the gate, with her two enormous dogs, Sugar and Sweet. When the door opened, and Hound Dog saw *them* – well. It turned out he *was* the crazy guard dog kind of dog after all.

With a ferocious snarl he went hurtling down the path, and with a volley of barks he hurled himself at Sugar and Sweet. Of course, he just bounced off the gate, but that didn't stop him. He picked himself up and hurled himself at the gate again. It was about three times as high as Hound Dog, but he caught on to the top with his front paws and by scrambling with his back legs he managed to get himself up. Then he flew at Sugar and Sweet.

Now, Sugar and Sweet are huge and very scary-looking. They are the kind of dogs you expect to see patrolling fences or guarding the Prime Minister. Both of them are way, *way* bigger than Hound Dog.

But that didn't make any difference to Hound Dog. He barked and snapped at them and it was as clear as anything that he was saying in dog language: "Get Off My Turf – This Place Is Mine!"

"Come here, Hound Dog!" I yelled, waiting for Sugar and Sweet to gobble him up.

But they didn't gobble. They just looked at him, gave a little whine, put their tails between their legs and tried to run away!

They were dragging Susie after them, while Hound Dog was nipping at their heels like a sheepdog rounding sheep, and Susie was shrieking, "Get your dog off!" And to make matters worse, Wild Thing decided to join in. She went chasing after Sugar and Sweet too, yapping at the top of her voice.

I'll tell you, for a dog that spends so much time snoozing on the sofa and eating ham, Hound Dog is pretty speedy. It took both me and Dad to catch him. Meanwhile, Zach and Bonnie grabbed Wild Thing by the back of her T-shirt and hauled her away from the action.

Dad wiped his forehead with one arm. "Wow! Owning a dog is harder than I thought."

Once Sugar and Sweet had gone home, though, Hound Dog behaved pretty well. Bonnie and Zach thought he was great, and fed him loads of treats, and watched him do his tricks (or refuse to do his tricks). When he settled down for a snooze at last (on the sofa, with Wild Thing curled up in his basket), Bonnie and Zach came upstairs to my room.

Bonnie's my very best friend and we're in the same class at school. Zach is a year older, but as I play saxophone in his band, along with his friends Big Sam, Little Sam, Henry and Dylan, we always have lots to talk about.

"I've got something to show you," said Bonnie.

"Take a look at this!"

She handed me a brightly coloured leaflet.

CHILDREN'S TALENT COMPETITION

Are you a star of the future?

Are you bright, talented and aged 6-13?

Can you sing, dance, act or play a musical instrument?

Or do you have a special talent of your own?

Enter the **Children's Talent Show** for

a chance to appear on TV!

Parental permission required.

"Just think, Kate – what an amazing opportunity!" Bonnie declared. "I just knew I had to show you!"

I didn't think it was amazing. As I read the form, I felt like a frog was leaping around in my stomach. I *hate* things like this. I mean, I love music – I get that from Dad I guess, and I can play the saxophone and guitar pretty well for my age – but I hate getting up on a stage and performing. It's something about all those faces. I can just about manage it with the rest of the band, at school, but it makes me feel all nervous and shaky.

Still, it was really nice of Bonnie to think I could do it. A big compliment. I'd have to let her down gently.

"That's really kind of you—" I began, but Bonnie interrupted me.

"So *I'm* going to enter. Isn't it exciting?"

"Oh," I said, taken aback. "But. . ."

"But what?"

"What can *you* do?"

It was a reasonable question, I thought. I mean, Bonnie is fantastic at football, and she can draw brilliant mermaids, and hoot like an owl – but she is not renowned as a star of the stage.

Bonnie glared at me. "*Sing*, of course!"

"Oh," I said again.

"You know I have a great voice."

I know Bonnie has a *loud* voice. *Loud* is not exactly the same as *great*.

In that respect Bonnie is a bit like Wild Thing. Dad reckons their voices could both break glass at fifty paces.

Luckily Zach intervened. "There's also a section for group acts. See – on the back. I was thinking our band could enter. What d'you think, Kate?"

"Umm . . . I'm not sure," I muttered.

I was torn. I picked up the leaflet again. This time I noticed something else across the top. "Look – all the money is for the Dog Rescue Trust. They're organizing it."

"Yeah," said Zach. "That's how we know about it. Mum's a big supporter."

"I think Hound Dog came from the Dog Rescue Trust. Wes went there and picked him out."

"That's what they do," said Zach. "They find new homes for dogs like Hound Dog."

He'd found my weak spot. I could just imagine all the poor homeless dogs, gazing at me with their big, soulful eyes. Even so . . . could I face it?

At that moment Hound Dog came in – or rather, Wild Thing did, thumping on the door and not waiting for an answer, and Hound Dog followed her.

"Don't just barge in!" I said.

"I'm getting some dirty clothes," said Wild Thing, heading towards my laundry basket.

I was a bit surprised, but I assumed that Dad was doing laundry, and had sent Wild Thing to get the clothes. So I turned back to Zach and Bonnie.

"I don't know. . ."

"Oh come on, Kate," Zach urged. "We can't do it without you."

Hound Dog gave a little whine and wagged his tail. And that made up my mind.

"OK, then!" I said quickly.

"Yay!" said Zach.

"I'm afraid I won't be able to play with the band *and* sing," said Bonnie importantly. "You'll just have to manage without me."

To be honest with you, Bonnie doesn't do much in our band anyway except bang a tambourine – usually out of time. I caught Zach's eye, and I could tell he was thinking the same thing. Neither of us said anything.

That's when I became aware of Wild Thing, going through my laundry basket.

"Hmm . . . that's *quite* smelly . . . that's *not* so smelly . . . that's *very* smelly. . ." she said, as one by one she held up a piece of my clothing and took a big sniff. Then she'd chuck them over her shoulder. All my underwear was piling up on the rug, and as I watched, horrified, Hound Dog settled himself down on it and nestled in with a contented sigh, as if to say, "Here's a nice cosy place to have a snooze".

"These will do – yes, they're good and smelly," Wild Thing announced then, holding up a pair of my pants. They were a really old pair, and actually had little fairies on them. I felt myself burning up with embarrassment.

"Wild Thing – *what are you doing?*"

"I need these. I'm teaching Hound Dog tracking."

"Tracking?"

"Yes. *Tracking*. I'm going to hide the clothes. Hound Dog's got to sniff them out!"

I stared at her, speechless with horror.

"I've already got some of Dad's stinky socks," Wild Thing went on. "They smell like old cheese. And these" – she waved my pants like a flag – "are just right too!"

I felt like the floor was going to swallow me up. I mean, WHY does she do these things? WHY? In front of my *friends*? In front of Bonnie, who sometimes makes fun of me, and Zach, who is older, and kind of cool if you want to know the truth? *Why* do I have such an embarrassing sister?

"Get out!" I shrieked, rushing at Wild Thing.

"Can I take your knickers?"

"No, you can't!"

I shoved Wild Thing out on to the landing. Hound Dog got up to follow her. "Hey, you just leave that, buster!" I said, as he tried to carry off some of my underwear in his mouth.

Bonnie and Zach were shaking. They had their lips squeezed shut, but their shoulders were wobbling. They were trying hard – I could tell – not to laugh. Suddenly it burst out. Bonnie's giggle was an *I-just-can't-help-it* squeaky kind of giggle, and Zach's was a big old snorty *Isn't-Wild-Thing-daft* kind of a giggle.

"Hey!" I said. But then, I couldn't help it – I was laughing and snorting too.

"Your sister is crazy!" Zach said, wiping his eyes.

"And your dog!" gasped Bonnie.

I made them promise not to say anything about it to anyone. They did, too. They are true friends, because we all knew it would have made a great story at school or to the band. But they both knew I really, *really* didn't want them to.

"We do understand what it's like for you," Zach told me. "After all, we've got Harris to put up with. Since he's turned fourteen it's just like having a gorilla living in the house."

After Zach and Bonnie had gone home, Wild Thing picked up the talent show leaflet that Bonnie had left behind on the kitchen table.

"What's this?"

I explained.

Wild Thing got that look on her face. The look that means she's thinking. It *always* sends shivers down my spine.

Wild Thing said, "*I* could be in a talent show."

"Doing what?" I asked.

"Being a Rock Star. I could wear my Rock Star outfit. I could wear my purple wig and my silver wedgey boots!"

Luckily, it wasn't going to happen. "Sadly," I said, "you can't be in the talent show because you aren't old enough. See, it says here you have to be over six."

"Not fair!" said Wild Thing.

She was really cross, and went to sulk under the kitchen table with Hound Dog. After a while I heard rasping sounds. I peered down. Guess what? Hound Dog was gnawing at one of the table legs – and so was my little sister!

"What do you think you're *doing*?"

Wild Thing said, "Well, he likes it. So I thought maybe it tastes good. But it just hurts my teeth."

"That's because *you're* not a dog."

And I managed to get them both to stop chewing the furniture before Dad saw.

7

Wild Thing didn't give up on her plan of teaching Hound Dog to track. I discovered that the next morning when I looked out of the kitchen window and saw Dad's boxer shorts hanging from the bird table.

Over the next couple of days I found: my school socks behind the Cheerios, my PE shirt in the bath, my shorts behind the wheelie bins, and, worst of all, one of Dad's smelly socks *in my homework folder*. All my friends fell about laughing when I pulled it out in class.

"This has got to stop!" Dad announced. He was annoyed because when Harris, Bonnie and Zach's big brother, had come round for his first guitar lesson and Dad had gone to fetch his guitar, he had found a pair of Wild Thing's tights wrapped round the neck of it. It had taken him ages to untangle them. (Dad had agreed to give Harris lessons to make up for Hound Dog attacking Sugar and Sweet.)

"Hound Dog *likes* to track!" Wild Thing squawked. "He's going to be a famous tracker."

"I'd have a lot more sympathy with that," Dad told her, "if Hound Dog ever *found* any of the things that you hid. But he doesn't. He couldn't be less interested. It's me and Kate who end up playing Hunt The Sock."

Luckily Harris just thought it was funny. He could hardly stop laughing.

He's OK, is Harris, although I'd been a bit taken aback when he first turned up on the doorstep. I hadn't seen much of him lately, and he'd really changed. He used to be cheerful and chatty – a bit like Zach. But now all his hair was hanging over his face, and his shoulders slumped, and he sort of shambled along with his guitar slung over his back and his arms dangling. Zach was right – he did look like a gorilla. And whatever anybody said to him, he just grunted.

I asked Dad later what was wrong with Harris, and Dad explained that nothing was wrong with him, he had just turned into a teenager. So that was OK. I guess. I mean, I hope I don't slouch and grunt and look like a gorilla when *I'm* a teenager.

But that wasn't the main problem. It wasn't his playing either – which Dad says is not bad for his age. It was Hound Dog. As soon as Harris started playing, he howled. And howled. And howled.

Even when Dad stuck him outside in the garden, he wouldn't stop.

Then Wild Thing joined in. "Ahooooooooooh!"

So Dad put *her* in the garden too.

Harris wasn't upset though. He just laughed. (A grunty kind of laugh – but definitely a laugh.) And the next time he came round for his lesson, Dad said to him, "Tell you what, Harris, I've found you a song to play by a famous guitarist called Howlin' Wolf. You know what they say – if you can't beat them, you might as well join them!"

The following Saturday Wild Thing and I were lounging around in our pyjamas, eating bowls of sugary cornflakes and watching morning TV. Or rather, I was lounging. Wild Thing was hunkered down in Hound Dog's basket with her bowl of cornflakes in front of her. The only problem was that it meant her breakfast was at the same level as Hound Dog, who reckoned he liked sugary cornflakes too. Wild Thing had her arms wrapped round the bowl, but you could tell as soon as he saw a chance, he was going to be right in there.

Then Dad came in. "Guess what we're doing this morning?"

Wild Thing and I looked at him.

"Watching TV and eating snacks?" I suggested. "Like we're doing?"

"Going to join the circus," said Wild Thing. (I wish she *would* go off and join a circus.)

"Wrong," Dad said. "It's a beautiful morning, and we're going to take Hound Dog to the park."

I groaned. "Why?" I asked. "We *always* do this on Saturdays mornings."

"Yes," Wild Thing agreed. "Saturday morning is telly morning!"

"*Not* now we have a dog," said Dad firmly. "Dogs need exercise."

He was right, of course. I knew Hound Dog needed his daily walk. Reluctantly, I stood up.

"No!" howled Wild Thing, not budging an inch. "Hound Dog wants to watch telly too!"

"Nonsense," said Dad. "He's just longing for a run in the park. Aren't you, boy?"

I suppose Hound Dog was meant to jump up eagerly and go and find his lead. But he didn't even look round. He was still watching Wild Thing's cereal like a fox watching a rabbit. He was drooling.

"See?" said Wild Thing.

"We'll all enjoy it once we get out," Dad replied.

"*I* won't," said Wild Thing. But Dad had made up his mind.

I was already dressed and waiting when Wild Thing appeared at the top of the stairs.

"Wild Thing! You can't go like that!"

"Why not?"

"Because you're wearing a swimsuit!"

"I want to go swimming with the ducks!"

Dad said there was going to be no swimming, with or without ducks, and she was to go and put on her jeans and T-shirt immediately. We went to wait on the front path with Hound Dog.

Eventually, she reappeared. She was wearing her jeans, top . . . and *my* inline skates. The ones I was given last Christmas. I only realized this when she came rolling down the path towards us at top speed.

"Stop!" I yelled.

"I can't stop!" yelled Wild Thing.

"Use your brake!"

But it was too late. Wild Thing went cannoning

into Dad, and they both ended up in a rose bush while Hound Dog ran round and round them, barking and winding them up in his lead.

"Ouch," said Dad, sucking his thumb.

"Those are my skates!" I yelled.

"It's good to share," said Wild Thing, untangling herself. "Miss Randolph told us that at school."

"*Sharing* doesn't mean just helping yourself to other people's things. Anyway, those skates are far too big for you."

"I've wedged them." (She had. With *my* socks, I discovered later.) "And I've had a brilliant idea," she went on. "I'm going to hold on to Hound Dog and he's going to pull me along."

Somehow, Wild Thing got herself upright. Then, before anybody could stop her, she grabbed hold of Hound Dog's lead and he set off down the path, pulling her behind him. Only, of course, she still couldn't stop herself.

"Help!" she squeaked, and Dad and I ran after her and grabbed her just before she collided with

Mrs Crabbe, our neighbour, who was walking along with her shopping. Mrs Crabbe already thinks we're mad, so she wasn't at all pleased.

Dad said that we were going to leave the skates at home. I was a bit annoyed about that (they are *my* skates – and I thought that Wild Thing's idea of being pulled along by Hound Dog looked like fun). But I cheered up when we got to the park. The sun was sparkling on the lake, the birds were singing their hearts out, and everyone was having a good time. Hound Dog liked it too, I could tell. He stood sniffing the air. Then Dad let him off the lead, and immediately he saw a big bunch of other dogs and ran after them.

"Look, he's playing," said Wild Thing as the dogs ran round, barking and chasing. She began to run about too.

"I suppose so," I said, a little doubtfully. "I mean, I think *he's* having fun. But – do you think they like him chasing them like that?"

"Of course they do," said Dad. "They're dogs. That's what they do."

"Hmm," I said.

It seemed to me that some of the other dogs' owners weren't too happy. They were shouting at their dogs to come back, and some of them were running after them, waving their leads. One of the owners, a man in a Sikh turban, came over to join us.

"Good morning," he said politely.

We said, "Good morning," too, and Dad added, "Good to see the dogs enjoying themselves, isn't it?"

"Well, actually," said the man, "I came here to ask if you would mind getting your dog back under control."

"Why's that?" asked Dad. "He just wants to play, like the others."

"Well, actually," said the man, "until he joined in, this was a dog training class!"

After we'd managed to catch Hound Dog at last, we dragged him off towards the woods, where he had a great time chasing squirrels. He didn't catch any – he didn't even get close – but that didn't seem to bother him. Wild Thing and I had a great time too, exploring the woods. I found three beautiful feathers and a white pebble, and Wild Thing found a muddy old branch full of wood lice and an old bird's nest which she made Dad carry for her. We even saw a woodpecker.

Then Wild Thing decided she was hungry, so we headed back to the lake and the ice cream van.

On the way we passed a bunch of people walking about in the undergrowth. They had long sticks. As we went past, one lady let go of a crisp packet and it fluttered towards us.

Wild Thing picked it up and held it out to the lady. She was about Gran's age, wearing a big pair of gloves and carrying a stick and a bin bag.

"You've dropped this," Wild Thing said.

"Well, thank you very much," said the lady, smiling and taking the crisp packet. "That's very kind of you." You could tell she was thinking *what a dear little girl*.

"It's bad to drop litter," Wild Thing told her.

"Oh, I agree—"

"So I'm going to tell the Park Keeper about you!"

The lady was a bit taken aback. She opened and shut her mouth. Then she said, "It *is* bad to drop litter. But you see, it was an accident. My friends and I are actually helping the park by picking all the litter up."

She held out her stick, and we saw that it had a pointy end, and she was using it to stab bits of litter and then put them in a big black bag.

"You're not very good at it, then, are you?" said Wild Thing in a loud voice.

Dad and me exchanged glances. The lady's smile was beginning to look a bit stiff. Like she was thinking Wild Thing wasn't such a dear little girl after all.

"Josephine," Dad began in a warning voice – but my sister took no notice.

"If you're no good at your job, you'll be sacked!" Wild Thing went on. "And a good thing too!"

Dad and me were really embarrassed.

"They can't sack me," the lady told my sister coldly, "because I'm a volunteer."

"What does that mean?" asked Wild Thing.

"It means she's doing it for free," I explained. "She doesn't get paid."

"I'm not surprised," Wild Thing replied, "when she's no good at it!"

At this point Dad and I managed to drag Wild Thing away. When we arrived at the lake, Dad bought me and Wild Thing ice cream cones with Flakes. "Not that you deserve one!" he told my sister. Wild Thing wanted him to buy Hound Dog one too, and while they were arguing about this, Wild Thing managed to drop her Flake. She gave a howl and tried to grab it, but before she could, Hound Dog whipped in there and wolfed it down in one bite.

"It's gone!" Wild Thing squeaked.

"Too bad," said Dad.

"Chocolate isn't good for dogs," I said. "I hope his tummy's OK."

Wild Thing was more concerned about her missing chocolate than Hound Dog's tummy. She kept nagging Dad as we all walked over towards the lake, while her ice cream started melting and running over her hand.

There were lots of birds on the lake – ducks and swans and geese – and lots of people feeding them. I wasn't sure it was a very good idea, going close with Hound Dog. So Dad put him back on his lead "just to be on the safe side".

For a few minutes we all stood watching the birds. It was very peaceful. Then one of the geese honked at Hound Dog, and the next moment he had flung himself right into the lake, trying to get at it. It all happened so quickly that Dad had no time to let go of the lead, so he was yanked in too.

SPLASH!

"Hooray!" yelled Wild Thing, as a great, curving wall of spray went all over us. "Daddy's in the lake!"

I shook my head. "They're absolutely soaking. We'll just have to – wait a minute. Wild Thing, what are you doing? Wild Thing, STOP RIGHT NOW!"

My little sister had walked a few steps away from the water. Taking no notice of me, she turned back round and began to run. Then with an enormous, happy shriek she leapt into the air . . . and straight into the lake!

And that was pretty much the end of our trip to the park.

8

A couple of days later, I was in the school playground at lunchtime, talking about the talent show.

Bonnie had told lots of people about it, and now several of our friends were planning to enter. Livy was going to play her recorder, and Jemima said she might have a go on her ukulele. I never even knew she played ukulele! Bonnie (or Bon-bon, as she now told us to call her) was telling everyone about her solo, while me and Zach and the rest of the band were discussing which songs we should play.

We were all having a great time . . . until I saw Miss Randolph coming straight towards me.

Uh-oh, I thought. Miss Randolph is Wild Thing's teacher.

"Oh *there* you are, Kate." She sounded really flustered. "I've been looking for you everywhere. We're having a bit of a problem with your sister."

I looked at Bonnie and raised my eyebrows. *Here we go again.* Why, whenever Wild Thing is difficult, do the teachers act like a) it's my fault and b) I'm the one to fix it?

"Come with me, dear," said Miss Randolph, "and let's see if *you* can talk sense into her."

Miss Randolph went clipping across the playground on her high heels, her flowery dress floating around her, and I trailed along behind. Bonnie came too, and so did all my friends. I guess the other kids in the playground must have wondered what was going on, because *they* started following too, and by the time we reached the Little Ones' playground we were quite a crowd.

"You see," said Miss Randolph, "it's time for the Little Ones to go inside now and do some lovely finger-painting, but Josephine – well – she won't come."

She pointed to where Wild Thing was crouched down in a muddy corner of the Little Ones' playground, under a tree.

I went over to her. "What's up, Wild Thing? Aren't you well?"

Wild Thing wrinkled her nose at me and made a snuffling noise.

"Everyone's waiting for you."

Wild Thing waggled her head.

"Miss Randolph's going to *really* blow her top if you just keep sitting there."

Actually this wasn't very likely – Miss Randolph is one of those sweet, gentle teachers who waft around smiling sweetly and calling children "dear" or "lamb" and cooing over them.

At that point, Miss Randolph came to join us. "Josephine! Now, dear – enough silliness. I want you to get up this minute!" She actually did sound quite fierce – for her. But I knew it wouldn't be fierce enough to shift Wild Thing.

Wild Thing opened her mouth and stuck out her tongue.

Miss Randolph gasped. I was beginning to wonder if there was something *wrong* with Wild Thing. I mean, it's not like her not to say anything. Usually she's got altogether *too much* to say.

Meanwhile, all the kids who had followed us were laughing. And all the Little Ones, who had already gone inside, were standing at the window with their noses pressed up against the glass, and their mouths wide open.

"What's Wild Thing done now?" somebody asked loudly. (Bonnie, I expect.)

Miss Randolph was still wittering on ("Josephine, I'm getting seriously annoyed, I'm warning you . . . I'm going to count to ten. . ."). I found myself staring at Wild Thing. There was something about the way she was sitting. She looked, well, not quite her usual self. I mean, she does act crazy, and Dad often calls her a wild animal, but she doesn't usually crouch down like that, or snuffle her nose, or pant with her tongue hanging out, and . . . *why* was she scrabbling about with that stick? She was actually *pushing it around with her nose.*

"Leave that dirty stick alone!" ordered Miss Randolph.

Suddenly, I had a revelation.

"Here, girl!" I called. I used exactly the same tone of voice we use with Hound Dog when we want to call him in from the garden.

It worked. Wild Thing came crawling towards me at top speed. She had the stick in her mouth and when she was level with me I said, "Drop it!"

Wild Thing let it fall to the ground.

"Sit!" I said firmly.

Wild Thing sat.

"Good doggy!"

I patted Wild Thing's head. Then I set off towards the building. As I went I slapped my thigh and said, "Heel!" Wild Thing kept up with me. When I reached the doors I stopped and Wild Thing stopped too. Her tongue was still hanging out of her mouth. "Good dog!" I said. "In you go now!"

Obediently, Wild Thing gambolled off, still on all fours, just as Miss Randolph came to join me.

Everyone watching began to clap. Some people were giggling, and Zach and the rest of the band began to cheer.

"What *is* going on?" demanded Miss Randolph.

"She's being a dog," I explained. "As long as you talk to her like she's a dog, she should be OK. If she won't do as she's told, you could offer her some ham, or a bit of sausage. That should do the trick. It does with our dog, anyway."

Miss Randolph gazed at me.

"Ham . . . sausage . . . I don't understand . . . *why* does Josephine think she's a dog?"

"I'm not really sure," I admitted. "But we've got a dog staying with us at the moment, and she really likes him. She often goes and sits in his basket. I think it's given her the idea that . . . well . . . that she'd like to be a dog."

Or maybe she really thought she *was* a dog. After all, with Wild Thing you never can tell.

Miss Randolph stood there for a moment with her mouth hanging open just like Hound Dog's when he sees a bit of sausage. "Of course, young children do have very vivid imaginations," she said weakly at last. "It's just role-play, really – we do a lot of role-play in class."

"I expect that's it," I said encouragingly.

"Well. . ." she said. "Well. . ." Then she turned and tottered after Wild Thing into the school.

Dad wasn't too happy when he found out about Wild Thing's new "phase", as he called it.

"I don't think it's *so* bad," I said.

"It's bad enough her doing it at home," Dad said. "I mean, every morning before breakfast, there they are, Hound Dog and Wild Thing. Watching TV together. Only the one that's sitting on the sofa is the dog! And the one curled up in a basket is my daughter!"

"She's not doing any harm."

"Earlier today, I caught her gnawing on Hound Dog's rawhide bone."

"Well, it's supposed to be good for *his* teeth, so it's probably good for *hers* too."

"Maybe. But it's not very hygienic. And look at her now!" Dad waved at the kitchen window. I went to take a look.

At first, as I gazed into our back garden, I couldn't see Wild Thing at all. Then I spotted her bottom sticking out from the long grass under the apple tree. "What's she doing?" I wondered aloud. "Is she hiding?" When Wild Thing was really little, she used to play hide-and-seek that way. She thought if *she* couldn't see *you*, then *you* couldn't see *her*.

"I think she's burying her bone," said Dad.

She was. Soon afterwards her head appeared. She was grinning, and even from this distance, I could see that her paws – sorry, hands – were covered in mud. Her face was muddy too. Dad gave another groan. Wild Thing saw us, but she didn't forget for a moment that she was a dog. She wiggled her bottom at us – I suppose that was the closest she could get to wagging her tail – and then she went scampering off round the garden on all fours, like a dog having a play.

"And meanwhile, do you know what the *real* dog is doing?" Dad asked me. "I'll tell you what he's doing – he's in the front room, sitting on the sofa, watching *Tracy Beaker Returns*." He shook his head.

Dad is usually quite chilled about Wild Thing – however awful she is. Usually it's *me* that she's driving crazy – not him. But somehow, this business of her being a dog was really getting to him.

"It's not so bad," I told him. "In fact, in some ways it's a good thing."

"What do you mean?"

"Watch."

I found a bit of leftover sausage in the fridge. Then I opened the back door. "Here, girl!" I called.

At once, Wild Thing came bounding towards me. When she reached me, I held out the sausage. Then I said, "Sit!"

Wild Thing hunkered down.

"Good girl!" I said, giving her the sausage. Then I turned to Dad. "See? She's *much* better as a dog. She actually does what she's told."

"I see what you mean," Dad admitted. "She's absolutely filthy though."

She was. She was covered from head to toe in grass and leaves. But then something else happened. Next door's tabby cat, Augustus, appeared on top of the fence. He jumped down daintily into our garden and went strolling across the lawn.

Wild Thing spotted him. The next moment she flung herself after him, barking ferociously.

Augustus went streaking away like lightning. He jumped on to the ivy, and went leaping up and over, into Mr and Mrs Crabbe's garden.

Wild Thing kept barking as she ran on all fours up and down the hedge, just in case Augustus dared sneak back through a gap. I had seen Hound Dog do exactly the same thing whenever *he* spotted a cat.

Dad gave a big sigh. To distract him, I got him to look at my maths homework. He was just explaining to me what I should be doing with the decimal point when the phone rang.

Dad picked it up.

"Hello," he said. "Oh, Mrs Crabbe. What can I do for you?"

From the high-pitched squawking that was coming out of the phone, I could tell that she was in a right old paddy about something. And when Dad finally got a word in edgeways, I soon guessed that – as usual – it was Wild Thing who was to blame.

"...Sorry to hear that ... Josephine's going

through a bit of a funny phase at the moment. It definitely won't happen again."

Dad hung up. His shoulders sagged. He looked at me with a hollow sort of expression on his face.

"Apparently," he said, "Wild Thing got through a gap in the hedge. She's been chasing that cat round Mrs Crabbe's garden."

"Well, that's not so terrible," I said.

"After she had chased the cat away," Dad went on, "Mrs Crabbe said Wild Thing had a good old scratch. Then she cocked her leg and peed against the apple tree."

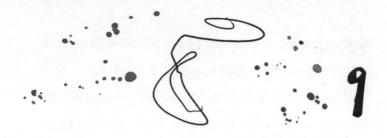

As I told Dad, it could have been a lot worse.

"I mean, what if Wild Thing hadn't needed to do a pee? What if she'd needed to do a—"

"Enough!" shouted Dad. "I've had enough!"

To be honest, I didn't mind Wild Thing being a dog (which was a good thing, as she didn't show any signs of stopping). So what if we had to put her bowl of cornflakes on the floor each morning. She ate them, didn't she? And she was probably no messier than if she ate them at the table – in fact, she was *less* messy, because, now she was a dog, she always licked up any cornflakes that she spilled. As I pointed out to Dad, that helped to keep the floor clean too.

Dad just muttered something about "living in a zoo" and "what's your grandmother going to say?" and then he stomped upstairs to his studio. I could hear him playing lots of moody guitar blues, all about how "my baby gone left me" the way he does when he's fed up.

I was a bit surprised Dad was so down in the dumps, because he doesn't usually take what Wild Thing does so much to heart. But I didn't find out the *real* reason he was so gloomy until later that afternoon. The phone rang, and I guess Dad was strumming away too loudly to hear it, because he didn't answer. So I picked it up. "Hello?"

"Hi, Katie, is that you?"

"Hey, Wes! Yes, it's me. How's the tour going?"

I was really excited to hear him. He'd sent us plenty of photos and messages from America (and we'd sent him plenty too, showing him how Hound Dog was doing) and it sounded as if the tour was going really well. The snippets on YouTube sounded great too – even if I didn't think Chris, their new guitarist, was a patch on Dad.

So I was really surprised when Wes replied in a really doleful voice, "It *was* going great . . . until this thing with Chris . . . and of course that changes everything. They're saying it will be in plaster for weeks, Katie . . . and you know yourself, top quality guitarists aren't thick on the ground. Can't *you* have a word with your dad, Katie, and make him change his mind?"

I felt like my ears were about to drop off, I was so amazed. Wes obviously thought I knew all about it – but I hadn't a clue. I didn't want to admit that though.

"Is Chris going to be OK?" I asked carefully.

"Yeah – eventually. What an idiot, though, tripping over his own guitar cable! Mind you, it could have happened to any of us. Still, he can't play the guitar with a broken arm. I know your dad says no way is he standing in . . . but Katie . . . I've called everybody . . . there's nobody else. . . I know he doesn't like to leave you girls, but it's only this once. Don't you think he might reconsider?"

"Well. . ."

"And the next gig is the Old Flamingo Club and he's always wanted to play there. Think of him playing some of his own songs at the Old Flamingo! It would be a dream come true. . ."

Wes went off on to a long spiel about all the guitar greats who had played at the Old Flamingo, but I wasn't really listening. I was thinking hard.

"Listen," I said, when Wes finally stopped talking. "Once Dad's made up his mind, it's hard to shift."

"*Try*, Katie," Wes urged me. "He won't listen to me, but he might to you."

After we'd hung up, I sat and thought for a bit. I thought about how gloomy Dad seemed. I reckoned he *wanted* to go. I mean, he always says he likes staying home with Wild Thing and me, and I know he does, most of the time, but . . . this was different. A chance to go to the US with the band, to visit some of his favourite places – places he'd heard about all his life. *Of course* he wanted to go. And would it really do Wild Thing and me any harm?

Only, if I rushed upstairs and told him so, would he listen?

I hesitated, then went to find Wild Thing.

Dad looked up in surprise when Wild Thing and I came bursting through his studio door. "Hey . . . what's up?"

"We have important things to discuss with you," I announced in my most important-sounding voice.

"Children's rights!" agreed Wild Thing, jumping up and down.

Dad raised an eyebrow. "*Children's* rights? I thought you were a dog?"

"Dog rights!" said Wild Thing quickly. She dropped down on to all fours. "Woof, woof!"

"The thing *is*," I said quickly, before Dad could get distracted by Wild Thing and her doggy ways, "everyone has rights, even children. . ."

"I hope this isn't about homework," Dad said.

"No, no—"

"Or another campaign to eat chocolate with every meal—"

"No, of course not," I said. "Will you just *listen*. Everyone in a family has rights, even you—"

"I'm glad to hear it," said Dad.

"And we reckon everyone in a family has a right to some time off. I go on sleepovers, don't I? And I went to Brownie camp last year. . ."

"I suppose so," said Dad. He was looking puzzled, wondering where all this was heading.

". . .And Wild Thing goes and stays over at Gran's sometimes, and once she went and camped out in Max's garden . . ."

"It was the best!" Wild Thing agreed extremely enthusiastically. "I ate twenty-four marshmallows! I was sick!"

". . . and so we reckon *you* deserve some time off too."

Dad frowned. "But I don't want to go to Brownie camp or sleep in the garden."

I took a deep breath. "No, but you could go to America with Monkey Magic now that Chris has broken his arm."

There was a long, long pause. "How did you

know about that?" asked Dad at last.

"It doesn't matter. The point is, Wild Thing and I have talked it over, and we've decided, haven't we, Wild Thing?"

"Everyone needs a break!" said Wild Thing, wagging her finger at him.

"We think that you should go!"

Dad looked from one to the other of us. He wasn't really used to us ganging up on him like this.

"But . . . who would look after you two?"

"We'll come too!" said Wild Thing, bounding up and down like a kangaroo (I guess she'd forgotten she was a dog for the moment).

"Absolutely not!"

"I knew you'd say that," I said. "But don't worry. Gran will take care of us."

"No way. Gran has enough to do . . . it's far too long . . . and she does work, you know. We can't ask her."

"We already have," said Wild Thing. "And she says yes."

Dad opened his mouth and shut it again. He looked just like a goldfish. "Are you sure she agrees?" he asked weakly at last.

"Yes," I said. "We called her on the phone just now. She thinks it's a great idea. It'll be good for all of us, she says, to have a change."

Dad did his goldfish act again. Then, at long last, he put down his guitar and held out his arms. Wild Thing and I ran over and hugged him.

"I don't know what to say. You girls have run rings round me. I shouldn't agree to this . . . I've always told myself I wouldn't . . . but – well – *thanks*, kids."

"I'm not a kid, I'm a dog," said Wild Thing. And she barked like crazy.

10

At the next band rehearsal, I told everyone about Dad going on tour. They were really excited. Zach hoped we'd be able to watch bits of it on YouTube. Bonnie asked, "Will you like having your gran look after you? She's quite strict, isn't she?"

"Not really," I said loyally. "I mean – she's stricter than Dad, but that's OK. She says she's looking forward to it, because she'll have a chance to sort Wild Thing out. She reckons there won't be any of that crazy 'I'm-a-dog' business while she's in charge!"

Everyone laughed. "Has Wild Thing peed on any trees lately?" asked Henry.

"No. But last night, when we were putting the dirty plates in the dishwasher, she and Hound

Dog were both on their hands and knees licking off the bits."

"Yeuch!" said Bonnie.

The boys fell around laughing.

"There's nobody like Wild Thing," said Zach.

"Yeah, she keeps you entertained," said Sam.

"You can say that again," I replied. "But I could do with a break sometimes. There's going to be lots of fireworks while Gran's trying to sort her out, I can tell you." I sighed.

"*I* know!" Bonnie jumped up so quickly she almost tripped over Big Sam's guitar case. "Why don't you come and stay with *us*? I'd *love* that! I've always wanted a sister. And you've always wanted to get rid of yours! It's perfect!"

I stared at her. "But what about your mum? Won't she mind?"

"Course she won't. Mum thinks you're great."

"I guess it would be easier for Gran too," I said slowly. "Just having one of us."

"Exactly. And we'll have so much fun!"

I could feel a big grin spreading across my face. "I think it's a brilliant idea!"

Bonnie gave me a huge hug. I hugged her back. "I'd *love* it!"

The boys chatted about their own stuff, while Bonnie and I made plans: we would sleep top-to-tail in Bonnie's bed, we would have midnight feasts, we would play tricks on Bonnie's brothers, we would cook hot dogs for tea. . .

I couldn't wait to tell Dad. When I got home he was in the middle of Harris's guitar lesson. So I stood there, hopping from foot to foot, until *finally* the lesson ended, and Harris slouched off in his usual gorilla-like way, and I blurted out my idea.

Only then I got a nasty shock.

"It won't do, Kate," said Dad. "It's not fair on Bonnie's mum. And it's not fair on Gran either."

"But it will be *easier* for Gran," I argued. "She won't have to look after me."

"Yes, but she'll have Wild Thing to deal with, and she might need your help. And what about Hound Dog?"

"Hound Dog can come with me."

"And live with Sugar and Sweet?"

I said nothing. There was nothing I could say. Every time Hound Dog met Sugar and Sweet he tried to start a fight.

Then I had an idea. "But I'll only be across the street," I pleaded. "I can still pop by and feed him and walk him each day."

Dad just looked at me. It was a long, serious sort of look. I began to get a funny feeling in the pit of my stomach. "But Gran's not moving in *here*, Kate," he said at last.

The funny feeling grew worse. "What do you mean?"

"I mean, you and Wild Thing are going to move in with Gran."

I stared at him in horror. "Noooooooo!" I wailed.

Dad looked solemn. "I thought you'd realize that's how it would be. Gran likes her own stuff around her. She's got her home office . . . her exercise bike . . . and she likes to cook in her own kitchen. She doesn't mind a couple of nights here, but this is much longer. So of course you're going there."

"But this is terrible!" I howled. It was, too. It was about the worst news I'd ever heard. Worst of all, it was *so unfair*. "If this is what comes of being a kind and considerate daughter . . . and wanting you to enjoy yourself . . . well then, I wish I'd never bothered!"

I stormed into the hall, past Wild Thing and Hound Dog – who were sitting on the stairs being guard dogs – and up into my room. I flung myself full-length on the bed. I couldn't believe it. *I just couldn't believe it.*

What got me most of all was that I'd been trying to be *nice* to Dad. In a book or a film, if you do a good thing for somebody, Fate usually makes sure that something good happens to you, too. But all Fate had done this time was turn round and give me a big punch on the nose!

Eventually there was a tap at the door, and Dad came in. He'd brought me a cup of hot chocolate, and two of those mint cream chocolate biscuits, all wrapped in shiny paper, that are my absolute favourites. At first I pushed them away, but eventually I unwrapped one and munched it sorrowfully.

"I'm really sorry about this, Kate," Dad said. "But it's too late for me to back out."

He looked really mournful – a bit like Hound Dog would if you took his bone away. I turned and flung my arms round him. "I *do* want you to go! It's just – it's just. . . "

I waved an arm at my bedroom.

My blue and white quilt. My shell collection that I'd brought back from the beach last summer. My saxophone on its stand. My guitar on *its* stand, and all my sheet music. My pinboard with pictures of my favourite bands. Blue Mouse, that I've had since I was tiny . . . my globe of the world that lights up . . . my dreamcatcher. . .

"I *love* my room," I said sorrowfully.

Then I thought about Wild Thing's room.

The big hole in the middle of her carpet that she'd made playing "Secret Tunnels". Her dolls – with their missing arms and legs and their eyes glued shut. The pile of torn-up newspaper that she'd made for "bedding" now that she was a dog. Her old sock collection. The seaweed that *she'd* brought back from the beach last summer, and which was now stuck in a dried-up mess to the chewing gum on the floor.

Because that was the thing. (Just in case you are thinking I'm making a terrible fuss about nothing.) There's nothing *wrong* with Gran's house really, except. . .

She only has one spare room.

Yes, that's right. One spare room. With bunk beds. Wild Thing and I would have to share.

At that moment, Wild Thing put her head round the door. She gave two loud barks. She was wearing her dog costume that her friend Max gave her. It's got brown fur with black spots, and big floppy ears.

"I'm looking forward to Gran's!" she announced, crawling into the room.

"Well, I'm not," I muttered.

"Kate's going to miss her own space," Dad explained. "And I want *you*, Wild Thing, to be very thoughtful and considerate."

Wild Thing put her head on one side. "OK, Kate. You can sleep on the bottom bunk."

"How does that help?" I growled.

"Cos then you don't have to worry about falling out."

Wild Thing beamed, as if she was being ever so generous, when actually she loves to sleep on the top bunk herself.

"I'm much more worried about *you* swinging about like an orang-utan and landing on my head!"

"Ooh!" Wild Thing's eyes lit up at this idea. Me and my big mouth!

"You've forgotten," said Dad. "Wild Thing's a dog now. She can't swing like an orang-utan. In fact, now she's a dog she can't even get on to the top bunk. Dogs can't climb ladders."

"*I* can," said Wild Thing at once. "I'm Wild Thing, the Amazing Circus Dog." Then she began racing round and round the room, barking and jumping up at things, until Dad got very stern with her, and made her go into her own room.

"It's not for long," said Dad, giving my shoulder a squeeze.

But to me it felt like *for ever*.

How on earth would I survive?

Gran came round to help us pack. I could hear her arguing with Wild Thing as I filled my own suitcase.

"Sock collection? You don't need a *sock collection. Or* a disco diva outfit. *Or* a wig. And what do you mean, you want to bring all that shredded-up newspaper. . ." Then she crossed the landing and started in on Dad. "You're taking *three* guitars but no smart shirts? How about some suncream?"

At least it meant that I could get on and pack what I wanted.

Then Dad helped us put all our stuff into Gran's car. Hound Dog sat between me and Wild Thing, clipped into his dog seat belt. "Are you *sure* you're going to be OK?" Dad asked for the fiftieth time.

"We're perfectly capable, aren't we, girls?" said Gran. "Now don't *worry*, Tom."

At that moment Dad's taxi pulled up to take him to the airport.

"Bye, Dad!" we shrieked. Hound Dog gave a mournful howl and Gran pulled into the street. We were off!

11

Gran's house is very modern and, unlike ours, always spick and span. Dad says even her house plants don't dare put a leaf wrong. You can't put down anything and leave it, the way you can at home, or Gran will tidy it away, or worse, chuck it in the bin. (Dad says when he was growing up, she was *always* throwing away the songs he wrote.)

On the other hand, it is nice sometimes to know exactly where everything is. And Gran has a TV in her kitchen, which we don't, so we can watch cartoons at breakfast. Plus her bath has these amazing Jacuzzi jets so it's like being in a whirlpool. And she gets much fancier breakfast cereal than we do, with maple-pecan chunks in it. So there are good things.

Of course, Wild Thing and I immediately started arguing about who would get the top bunk. Gran said she would toss a coin. Wild Thing yelled, "Heads!" and it was heads. "Not fair," I grumbled. "*I* was going to choose heads too." But it was too late.

Gran sent us up to unpack straight away.

"Now listen, Wild Thing," I said, as I put Blue Mouse gently on my pillow, "there's just one thing you have to understand. *Don't mess with my stuff!* Got that?"

"Don't want your stupid stuff!" Wild Thing yelled. She was busy bouncing up and down on the top bunk. The bunk beds were *swaying*, like a skyscraper in a tornado. Her suitcase was wide open on the floor, and all her stuff was strewn over the big rug. It was a lovely rug with pink and blue and green candy-stripes, but it was mainly buried under Wild Thing's possessions.

I quickly finished unpacking and left her to it. Luckily, Gran had said I could keep my saxophone and guitar in the living room, so there was less risk of Wild Thing destroying them. I put them on their stands, then went to find Gran.

She was in the kitchen, making cottage pie. Hound Dog was sitting at her feet staring soulfully at the minced beef.

"I'm making a healthy, home-cooked dinner for us all," Gran announced, flinging carrots into a pan. "In my opinion, it's time that Josephine – and all of you – ate more sensibly. There will be no Lucky Dips here. Kate, would you put some food down for Hound Dog? There's dog food in that cupboard."

I opened the door, then gaped at all the shelves piled high with shiny packets of dog food. I'd never seen so much dog food! I guess it must have been on Special Offer. (Gran's a great one for Special Offers.) But – they weren't his usual brand.

"Err – you know, Gran, Hound Dog only likes one kind of dog food. I thought Dad told you."

"Nonsense!" said Gran briskly. "I'm not

buying that organic stuff! It's five times the price of every other dog food. He's a *dog* – he'll eat what he's given."

"Oh."

I picked up one of the packets. It was labelled "Doggy Delight: Rabbit Chunks with Jelly". I opened it and emptied it into a bowl for Hound Dog.

It looked and smelt pretty disgusting. Still, Hound Dog was a *dog*. He had been known to eat ancient tuna sandwiches that he'd found under a hedge. Not to mention the raw eggs that he had lapped off the carpet the time that Wild Thing had decided to be a circus juggler. Maybe he'd like Rabbit Chunks.

He trotted over, sniffed at it – then snorted in disgust and went back to sit at Gran's feet.

"He'll eat it when he gets hungry," said Gran grimly.

I shrugged. We'd tried Hound Dog on all kinds of dog food – unsuccessfully. Of course, he did like eating *our* food – especially roast chicken dinner. And I had a feeling he would *love* cottage pie. But I wasn't about to argue with Gran. I could tell she was in one of her no-nonsense moods.

"Your dad lets that dog and that sister of yours run rings round him," Gran went on. "He's going to get a lovely surprise when he comes home and finds out how well they *can* behave!"

You can try, I thought.

Ten minutes later, Gran went up to our bedroom. She nearly blew a gasket. Wild Thing's stuff was *everywhere*.

"Right, Josephine, I want this all cleared up and put away *right now*. There'll be no cottage pie for you until it's tidy."

"Don't like cottage pie."

"Nonsense! And there'll be no playing in the garden, either, and no TV."

Wild Thing scowled. "I hate tidying. *You* help me!"

But Gran said Wild Thing was plenty old enough to do it herself.

I was very impressed with Gran's firmness.

Dad would have given in. I went off to practise my saxophone.

From upstairs, there was a series of thuds and shrieks, which I guessed was Wild Thing throwing her stuff around in a temper. Then there was a long silence, which I guessed was Wild Thing sulking. Finally there was the sound of her moving about the room. At long last, she yelled down the stairs, "Finished!"

Gran went upstairs to inspect. I followed. Hound Dog tried to follow, but Gran said, "No dogs upstairs!" and shut him in the kitchen.

Gran stood in the doorway to our room, hands on hips. She looked like a general surveying the field of battle.

"All done! All done!" Wild Thing chanted, jumping up and down.

We looked round. The beds were clear. The covers were pulled straight. The suitcases were empty. The furniture was neat. But the rug . . . what was up with the rug? It was all lumpy and bumpy. It looked like an army of moles had got into the bedroom and dug molehills all over the floor.

"Josephine," said Gran quietly, "This may come as news to you, but when I say *tidy*, I *don't* mean shove all your toys under the rug. Did you think I wouldn't notice?"

Gran and I went downstairs again, leaving Wild Thing howling with rage. "It took me ages to put them there!" she yelled down the stairs after us.

When teatime came, Wild Thing refused to eat her cottage pie. "Don't like it," she said, wrinkling her nose and stirring the meat around with her fork. "Want orange dinner!"

"What's orange dinner?" asked Gran.

"Err, Wild Thing's been learning about colours at school," I said. "And we've found sometimes she eats better if she can have food all one colour. She likes orange best."

"You mean," said Gran, "carrots, lentil soup, sweet potatoes, that kind of thing?"

"No!" said Wild Thing. "*Not* that horrible stuff! Cornflake cakes and nachos and hash browns and waffles!" Gran stared at her with an appalled look on her face. "Sometimes," Wild Thing went on, "I eat orange food all day!"

"But you eat cottage pie, too," I pointed out.

"From the supermarket," Wild Thing agreed quickly. *"This isn't the same."*

"It's my *home-made* cottage pie!" said Gran crossly. "It's much better than something you get from the supermarket!"

"Anyway, I'm a dog, and dogs don't eat cottage pie."

"I bet Hound Dog would if he had the chance," I said.

"Well, he's not getting the chance," said Gran. "I don't spend my time making home-cooked food – for dogs!"

To add insult to injury (Gran's words) Hound Dog wouldn't touch his new dog food either. From time to time he would go over and sniff at it, then turn and look at us with an expression on his face which said, clear as words, "What's this muck you've given me? I'm not eating this!"

It made me giggle. But Gran was Not Amused.

"The thing is he's not used to it," I tried to explain. "If you just gave him a *little* cottage pie—"

"I've had enough of this." Gran's voice was so barky she sounded a bit like a dog herself. "You" – she pointed at Wild Thing – "are a girl, and that" – she pointed at Hound Dog – "is a dog, and the sooner everyone gets that straight the better!"

I quietly finished my cottage pie (it was delicious) and Gran said I could leave the table. So I left them to it ("Won't eat it!" "Yes you will!" "No I won't!") and went to play my guitar.

I was feeling a bit gloomy, so I thought I'd play something sad, the way Dad does when he's low. I couldn't think of a song I knew that exactly matched my mood, but Dad had shown me some blues chords, so I played around with those, and even thought of some words to go with them. Soon I had invented a little blues song of my own.

I called it "Homesick Blues".

Even though it was sad, it did make me feel better, singing it.

Then Gran said it was bath time. I told Gran I'd have a shower later, as I wanted to watch TV, but Wild Thing decided to have a bath straight away. When I walked across the landing I could see her running the water, and emptying Gran's bubble bath into frothing Jacuzzi jets.

After that, all was peaceful, until suddenly I

heard a shout, then Gran yelling at the top of her voice, "What's that dratted dog doing in there? Get him out *this minute!*"

I raced up the stairs just in time to see Hound Dog charging out of the bathroom and across the landing, all covered in blue bath foam, while Wild Thing, still in the bath, shouted at Gran, "Why shouldn't he get in – dogs need washing too!"

I chased Hound Dog all round the house and finally caught him and rubbed him down with a bath towel. It really cheered me up. But my mood plummeted again at bedtime. Wild Thing kept wriggling about on her top bunk and dropping toys on my head, and she just *wouldn't* go to sleep. All her messing about kept *me* awake too. Gran had insisted that Hound Dog be shut up in the kitchen, and every now and then I heard him give a lonesome howl. Eventually Wild Thing dropped off, but by that time, *I* was wide awake. And Wild Thing must have got herself into a funny position, because she was snoring. *Really* loudly.

It's going to seem like the longest time ever until Dad gets back, I thought.

I really missed home and my own bed and all my things. I thought about Dad being in an aeroplane, high over the sea. I couldn't even call him. A tear trickled down my face and dribbled off the end of my chin. Another tear followed it.

With a gentle click, the bedroom door opened. I heard a soft *pad-pad-pad* across the rug. The next moment, a rough tongue licked my damp face. Then, the new arrival hopped up on to my bunk, turned around twice, and settled himself in a warm heap on my feet.

"Hound Dog!" I whispered. Somehow, he had got out of the kitchen. Gran was going to be *really* mad when she found out. But I wasn't about to tell her. I stroked Hound Dog's soft fur and listened to the sound of his tail beating against the duvet cover.

I felt a million times better. It wouldn't be *that* long! We'd survive – somehow.

12

"That sounded pretty good," said Zach. We all looked at each other and grinned. We were in the school practice room, where we'd just played through our first number for the talent show, and Zach was right – it was sounding good.

"Sorry, guys, but I think it would have sounded a lot better with my tambourine," said Bonnie. "It just gives it that extra pizazz."

The rest of us exchanged glances. To be honest, I don't think we really felt that a tambourine made much difference either way. I wondered if Bonnie was feeling left out.

"Well, you're welcome to play with us," I said. "It was you who said you couldn't. How is your solo going, anyway?"

I realized I hadn't heard Bonnie mention it

for ages – and there were only a couple of days now until the talent show. Of course, I didn't see as much of Bonnie now I was staying at Gran's. It wasn't that far away, but it wasn't like living on the same street either. We didn't walk back from school together, for one thing – I walked with Jemima instead. And Bonnie and Zach didn't drop round on their way to the skateboard park any more. And it wasn't as easy for me to take my saxophone round to their house to practise – which was one of the reasons why we were practising today at school.

"It's going fine, thanks."

I was about to ask more, but Henry said, "How're you getting on at your gran's, Kate? Is Wild Thing still pretending to be a dog?" He snorted with laughter.

"Yep. What's driving Gran crazy is she won't eat anything."

"How d'you mean?" asked Big Sam.

"Well, Gran keeps trying to feed her healthy

food . . . and Wild Thing says she's a dog and won't eat it."

At that moment, the door to the corridor opened and Miss Randolph looked in. "Ah – Kate, I was looking for you."

"Oh," I said. There was usually only one reason why Miss Randolph came looking for me: Wild Thing.

Miss Randolph came towards me. Then she bent low, close to my ear, as if she didn't want anybody to hear. Of course, this just made the rest of the band curious, and they all leant closer to listen. I wished Miss Randolph didn't wear such a strong perfume – it made me want to sneeze.

"Kate, your granny phoned earlier and left a message saying she was working late and couldn't pick up Wild Thing this afternoon, and that she'd arranged for a babysitter to pick her up instead. Which is fine, of course. But, err . . . I just wanted to double-check . . . is *this* really the babysitter your granny meant?"

She turned back to the open door and called, "Come in, you two."

Wild Thing and Harris came in from the corridor. Wild Thing was bouncing like usual, and Harris was slouching like usual. They looked like a baby kangaroo out for a walk with a gorilla.

I could see why Miss Randolph was worried. Harris doesn't look anything like the other childminders – who are usually nice, friendly ladies with toddlers in buggies and sensible shoes. Not grubby teenage lads with greasy black hair all over their face who grunt whenever they speak.

"'lo, Kate," Harris said (or rather, grunted).

"Hi, Harris," I said. "Yeah, he's fine, Miss Randolph. He's a friend of the family."

"He's my *brother*," said Bonnie indignantly. "Did you think he was a *kidnapper* or something?"

Miss Randolph blushed red and told Bonnie not to be rude. Then she clip-clopped out of the room again. Harris grinned. He didn't seem to mind at all that Miss Randolph thought he looked like a kidnapper.

"Wild Thing and me are off to walk Hound Dog," he grunted at me. "See you later."

"What are *you* all doing?" asked Wild Thing nosily.

"If you must know, we're practising for the

talent show," I told her. "Not that it's any of your business."

"*I'm* going to be in the talent show," said Wild Thing.

"Good for you," I said. I couldn't be bothered to argue with her. I knew she wasn't really.

Harris and Wild Thing left. But Wild Thing mentioning the talent show had reminded me of Bonnie's song again.

"So how *is* your song going, Bonnie?"

"My stage name is Bon-bon."

"All right then, so how is it going *Bon-bon*?"

"Wonderful. You're going to *love* it."

"Why don't you sing it to us, then?" Henry suggested. I guess the rest of the band was as curious as I was, because they all put down their instruments and said, "Yeah – go on, Bon – let's hear it."

"I'm shy," said Bonnie.

This was a bit of a joke, as Bonnie is about the least shy person I've ever met. I reckoned she just wanted to surprise us on the night.

Or maybe she wanted us to beg her. Still, we pointed out that she'd have to sing in front of lots of other people at the talent show, so she might as well get some practice. So Bonnie got up and smoothed down her skirt.

"This song is called 'I Will Always Love You'," she announced.

The boys made faces at each other. They don't like lovey-dovey songs. I didn't mind what the song was *about* – but as soon as she started, a shudder ran down my spine. The truth was, Bonnie sounded awful. Her voice was wobbling all over the place. Also, she started off too high, which meant that as the song got higher, she couldn't reach the top notes, and her voice began to squeak. I tried not to catch the others' eyes, but I could see Henry wince when she hit (or rather, *didn't* hit) the high notes.

I wished that I'd never, ever asked her about her song. Because now, somehow, I was going to have to convince her not to sing it.

Eventually the wailing and warbling stopped.

Then she looked round at us. "Well?"

Nobody said anything. The funny thing is, if she'd been good, then the boys would probably have teased her, saying she sounded like cats fighting, or the school fire alarm (boys are like that). But because she was so dreadful, they didn't know what to say. They just looked at the floor and said "Err" and "Umm".

"Well, Kate?" Bonnie asked.

"Errm," I said. "I know you tried really hard, but . . . I'm just wondering if that song is a bit too . . . difficult?"

I knew immediately that I hadn't put it the right way. Bonnie turned bright red. "You pig!"

"Bonnie!"

"You're supposed to be my best friend!"

"I *am* your best friend!"

"So why are you being horrible?"

"I'm only trying to help!"

"No, you're not!" Bonnie's face crumpled. "I know what it is! It's because you don't like me any more!"

I was stunned. "Of course I like you!"

"No you don't . . . it's all Jemima this, Jemima that . . . you never have time for me."

"That's just because of living closer to Jem now—"

"And now you're saying I can't sing!"

There were actually tears running down Bonnie's cheeks. The boys shifted their feet with embarrassment. I felt terrible. Really terrible. I'd never meant to leave Bonnie out.

"Bonnie – you're my best friend – course you are!"

"Promise?"

"Promise! And – whatever song you want to sing, I'll support you."

"Good," said Bonnie, sniffing. "Because that's the one I'm singing!"

13

I got a bit of a shock when I asked Gran what we were having for dinner that night. I expected her to say "vegetable soup" or "onion quiche" or "fish pie". Instead she said, "Hmm, now, let me see . . . sausage rolls, nachos, waffles, potato wedges, cheesy bites. . ."

I stared at her in surprise. "But I thought you said those kinds of things weren't healthy?"

To my astonishment, Gran turned around and sat down at the kitchen table. She looked at me, and there was real desperation in her eyes.

"I'm at the end of my tether, Kate. Josephine won't eat a blessed thing! I don't want your dad coming home and finding that she's getting rickets and her teeth are falling out! So tonight we're having orange dinner. I know it's not very healthy – but does it matter, so long as she eats something?"

I patted Gran's arm. "I'm sure it's just a phase she's going through."

Gran sighed, picked up Hound Dog's bowl and reached into the cupboard for his dog food. "I've already given way and bought the dog that expensive food he prefers. We've got loads of those Doggy Chunks left too – such a waste. And now orange dinner!"

I helped Gran put our food on the table. It was certainly making *my* mouth water. Then Wild Thing came waltzing in, with Hound Dog close behind her. "I like Harris," she announced. "I want him to babysit me every day."

Gran snorted. "He's a nice enough lad. I just hope he hasn't been letting you eat chocolate and crisps. I want you to make a good tea for once, Josephine. I've bought some of your favourite things."

Wild Thing glanced at the table. "Not eating it!" she announced.

Gran went very red.

"Go on, Wild Thing," I urged my sister. "Gran's bought all this specially for you. You know you love" – I picked up the nearest plate – "potato wedges."

Wild Thing shook her head. "I'm a *dog*," she explained kindly, "and dogs don't eat potatoes."

Gran gave a kind of groan. She was really suffering, I could tell. Although, to be honest, Wild Thing looked perfectly healthy. Her skin glowed, her cheeks were pink as apples, her eyes sparkled, her teeth were white and her coat (I mean hair) was glossy and shining. She looked as if she were bursting with health and vitamins. If she were a dog, I reckoned she could appear on a dog food advert.

And that's when I suddenly got suspicious. I sat for a moment, thinking.

"Wait a minute," I said. *"Wait a minute!"*

I got up and walked over to the cupboard. The cupboard that was packed full of Doggy Chunks. Rabbit-flavour chunks, lamb-flavour chunks, liver-flavour chunks, all mixed in with meaty jelly. All bursting (so the packets said) with protein and vitamins.

I opened the cupboard door. The shelves were still piled high with dog food packets.

But . . . there was one important difference. When I looked more closely, I realized most of the packets weren't full of dog food any more. Most of them were empty.

"Yum, yum!" said Wild Thing.

Gran wanted to take Wild Thing straight to the doctor – even the hospital – to be checked out. But I thought it was a bit late to worry. Wild Thing had obviously been eating dog food for days and days. And it hadn't done her any harm. In fact, she looked really well on it.

"Full of healthy goodness," I said, reading the side of the packet. "And twenty-one vitamins!"

"Yes," Gran retorted, "good for dogs!" Then she turned on Wild Thing. "What possessed you?"

"I'm a dog," Wild Thing wailed. "Dog food's what dogs eat! Anyway – I like chunks."

"No more," Gran told her. "It may not have done you any harm, but from now on, I want you to eat sensible, healthy, HUMAN meals!"

In the end, Wild Thing agreed. She had to, really. Gran took the remaining packets of Doggy Chunks round to Sugar and Sweet that very evening, and as for Hound Dog's new food, she put that on the very top shelf of the very highest cupboard so that Wild Thing couldn't get at it. And just in case she tried, Gran counted every single tin, so she would know at once if any of them were gone.

I don't think Wild Thing was that upset, to be honest. The following night, we had Gran's home-made lasagne with garlic bread and peas, and apple pie to follow.

Wild Thing had three helpings!

14

Finally, the day arrived. The day of the talent show!

Dad sent me an email that morning.

Very best of luck – I know you'll do brilliantly, it said. *I'll be keeping my fingers crossed for you, and so will all of Monkey Magic. I've asked Gran to video the show, so I'll be able to watch it afterwards. Remember – you've got to be brave in the music business! Lots of love – Dad. XXX*

It brought a lump into my throat, reading it. I've never done anything that big without Dad being there. But I knew he was having a great time. And he'd be home in a week.

Only sometimes, a week can seem like a long time.

Gran was coming, but she wouldn't be there

until the very start of the show. Even though it was a Saturday, she had some work to do first. "But don't worry, I won't be late. I promise. And I've arranged for you to go early with Zach and Bonnie."

"What about Wild Thing?"

"Harris is going to take her there on the bus. She seems to think it will be a wonderful adventure."

Gran left, wearing her smart work clothes. I was feeling more nervous by the moment. I could hardly eat anything, and I spent forever deciding what to wear, even though I wasn't planning on anything fancy – just jeans and a simple top. I had my saxophone ready ages before it was time to go. At long last, I heard the hoot of the horn, and saw Zach and Bonnie waving at me out of the back of their big SUV.

"Remember to walk Hound Dog!" I yelled at Harris and Wild Thing, who were playing *Minecraft*. Then I slammed the front door and went running down the path.

I clambered into the back of the car. Zach was wearing jeans and a black top, like me. Bonnie, though – wow! She was wearing a grey silk dress covered in sequins, with an enormous bow on one shoulder, and shiny silver shoes, and as for her hair, I guess she must have used curling tongs, because all the frizz was gone, and it was all arranged in waves round her face, fixed with a velvet bow. She wearing a tonne of make-up too – red bow lips and false eyelashes.

"What do you think?" she asked, fluttering the eyelashes.

"Err . . . amazing," I said politely.

The talent show was taking place in a hotel. It was a lot bigger, and fancier, than we had expected. Bonnie and Zach fell silent, and we all just stared around us with big eyes, as the manager showed us through to the Grand Ballroom. There was lots of gold paint and red velvet everywhere, and enormous flower displays, and also some pictures of dogs, because, of course, the whole event was in aid of the Dog Rescue Trust. The chairs (which all had satin bows on them) had been arranged in rows facing a big curtain. Behind this curtain was the stage, with more enormous flower arrangements on each side, and a door at the back leading through to the performers' area.

Susie said she would see us later – from the audience. Then she waved and disappeared.

There were loads of people backstage already. Henry and the two Sams came to meet us, and Dylan joined us soon afterwards. There were people wearing tutus – and carrying trombones – and practising close harmony singing. One boy was wearing a top hat and tails and twirling a silver-topped cane. A bunch of girls was tap-dancing in one corner. There were a couple of other bands too. They were older than us, and one of the guitarists was practising riffs – he was *good*.

"There's a lot of people," said Bonnie in a small voice.

"Of course there are – what did you expect?" I may have sounded more snappish than I meant to – but the truth is, I was feeling scared too. We began to get ready, and then a lady with a clipboard came round to show us the "running order". Our band was on first – and Bonnie's song was on towards the end.

We walked out into a sea of faces. The whole ballroom was packed, with row after row of people all sitting tight together in those velvet chairs. They clapped as we came out, but I could still hear my heart going *thumpetty-thud*. To be honest, if I hadn't been with the rest of the band I'd probably have turned and fled. We all glanced at each other and exchanged nervous smiles.

Zach is good at staying calm in a crisis. He turned to us and went, "A one-two-three..."

We all agreed afterwards that it wasn't our best performance. Dad always says it's hard, being the opener, and I think he's right. We did OK, but I played some wrong notes, and so did Dylan and Zach, and Little Sam definitely had a cold, because his voice wasn't as strong as usual. The crowd clapped like mad though.

"Hey, they really liked it," whispered Zach.

I soon forgot all about our performance, though, because when we got backstage, I got the most horrible shock.

There, standing in the middle of all the other performers, wearing a white trouser suit with pink sequins and sequin-covered boots was – Wild Thing. She had a grin like a slice of watermelon.

And just in case I'd hoped that it was some other five-year-old hidden under that shocking-pink wig and glittery sunglasses, there was no mistaking Hound Dog. Even though he was wearing a bright pink leopard-print collar with glittery fake jewels and bright pink sunglasses too!

"What are you *doing* here?" I hissed.

"I'm taking part in the talent show, stupid," said Wild Thing.

I was absolutely gobsmacked. At last I bleated, "You're too little!"

"Am not," said Wild Thing.

"You are so! It says on the form you have to be over six."

"You've got to be brave in the music business," my sister told me.

"You mean you lied on the form!"

My eye caught Harris, who was standing just behind her, holding his guitar. "Why did you bring her?" I demanded. "You're meant to be in the audience."

"Chill out, Kate," said Harris. "Our act is gonna be great."

I couldn't say any more because at that moment the lady with the clipboard came over and told Wild Thing that she was up next!

I groaned. I wasn't sure what to do, to be honest. I suppose I could have told the lady that Wild Thing was too young. But then there would have been a terrible row and besides, I don't like to tell tales. Anyway, before I could make up my mind, the lady was ushering them on to the stage.

As she went she turned to me, smiling, and said, "Aren't they *adorable*?"

"Adorable! Huh!" I said. She looked shocked.

Zach grabbed hold of my arm. "Come on, Kate – let's watch the show."

We couldn't go out into the audience, but there was a special TV monitor set up backstage so all the performers could watch the other acts. We gathered round in time to hear the man with the mike announce, "Next up – the Wild Things!"

The Wild Things! Oh no.

But Wild Thing didn't appear immediately. Instead, Harris walked on to the stage. He was playing "Great Balls of Fire" on his guitar. Just as he got to the crescendo of the song – Wild Thing came racing in, and went straight into the splits!

The audience seemed a bit stunned. They weren't sure how to react. Wild Thing didn't worry though. She got up and bowed, just as if they'd given her a standing ovation. Then she turned and yelled, "Here, boy!" and Hound Dog trotted on to the stage.

When they saw Hound Dog, with his shades and glittery collar, some of the audience, mainly the female ones, went, "Awwww! Isn't he *cute?*"

Wild Thing said to the audience: "Now Elvis is going to perform some tricks."

She picked up a hoop. (I reckoned it was her hula hoop, covered in tinsel she'd stolen from the Christmas decorations box.) "Now Elvis will jump through this hoop. Here, boy!"

I don't know whether Hound Dog had ever jumped through a hoop before in his life. He'd certainly never done it when *I'd* been there. Of course, maybe Wild Thing had been teaching him, secretly. If so, then it must have been all the spectators that put him off. Or maybe it was being called Elvis, instead of Hound Dog. Because he didn't jump through the hoop. He didn't even try.

He just sniffed at it, then sat down, right in the middle of the stage.

Some of the audience were puzzled. Others thought it was funny. There were ripples of laughter across the room.

Wild Thing got very cross. "ELVIS, JUMP!" she shouted. And when he still wouldn't, she yelled, "BAD DOG!"

"Hey, try this," said Harris, taking something out of his pocket and handing it to Wild Thing.

I guess it was some kind of snack. Wild Thing held it in one hand, and the hoop in the other, and yelled, "Come on, Hound Dog – jump!" She waved the snack enticingly at Hound Dog.

Hound Dog must have liked the look of the snack. He got up, trotted across the stage, *round* the hoop, and sat down in front of Wild Thing.

Wild Thing was so cross that she threw the hoop across the stage. It almost hit one of the big flower arrangements. She told Hound Dog, "No snack for you!" Hound Dog yawned and scratched his back leg. Then he stood up and neatly helped himself to the snack from Wild Thing's hand before she had time to stop him.

By now, most of the audience were laughing.

Then Harris began to play my sister's favourite

song. It's the one called "Wild Thing" that my dad wrote, years ago, and that she believes is all about her.

She's a demon child
She's not meek and mild
She's wild!
Oh yeah...

She can bite
Oh yeah and she can fight!
She'll give you a fright!
Oh yeah!

She's wild, wild, wild!
Yeah!
Oh she's wild, wild, wild...

Wild Thing bounded around the stage, and every now and then she'd yell, "Come on, Elvis – join in!" About halfway through the song, he decided that he would. First he stood up and shook himself. Then Wild Thing boogied over to him and held out her hands, and Hound Dog actually got up on his back legs and let her hold his front paws, and boogied around with her.

I reckoned some of the audience would be taken away on *stretchers* soon, they were laughing so much.

"Hey, they're a hit!" said Zach.

Hound Dog soon got bored of boogying, though, and sat down and had another scratch while Wild Thing finished the last verse. She did a running splits again to finish – and just managed to stop before she went hurtling off the end of the stage. Then she got up to take her bow. The audience was going wild. They just loved my sister and her crazy dog. Wild Thing bowed again and again. She even blew kisses to the crowd.

Hound Dog wasn't impressed. He finished scratching, gave a big yawn and trotted across the stage. When he reached the giant flower arrangement, he cocked his leg and peed on it!

Well, I guess it probably looked like a tree to him.

There were howls of laughter. Everyone was pointing at Hound Dog, and Wild Thing turned to look where they were pointing. "Bad dog!" she yelled and rushed up to him, shaking her finger. Hound Dog must have thought it was a game. He barked and rushed round and round the flower arrangement. Wild Thing ran after him. Every time she was about to catch him, Hound Dog would wait until the last moment and spring away. He was really enjoying himself, you could tell.

At last Harris and the man with microphone and the lady with the clipboard managed to round up Wild Thing and Hound Dog and get them off the stage. The audience were hysterical. I reckoned Hound Dog probably wasn't the only one who'd wet himself!

15

I was so cross with Wild Thing, I decided the best thing was to try to pretend she wasn't there. I watched the next acts on the TV monitor, and I soon became so interested in the rest of the show that I was able to relax and – *almost* – forget about my sister.

There were some great acts, and after we heard the next band play, we knew that we had no chance of winning. "They're amazing," Zach said – and they were. The guitarist did a solo that made me gasp, and the girl that was singing almost *did* sound like a professional singer. I discovered that while I was glad that I'd been brave enough to take part, I didn't mind losing either – not to people who were so much better.

"And after all, they're a lot older," I said to the rest of the band.

"Yeah," Henry agreed. "It gives us something to aim at."

Then came an interval, where all the performers were brought ice creams and drinks. That was fun. I also went and peered through the door on to the stage to see if I could spot Gran. I couldn't – but then, there were so many people milling around, I might easily have missed her. I went backstage again, and chatted to the rest of the band. I made sure to ignore Wild Thing – not that she cared. Everyone kept fussing over her, and even asking for her autograph. As for Hound Dog – somebody had brought him a plate of sausage rolls, and he was in Doggy Heaven!

Then the show started again. There was a ballet dancer, the violinist (she was quite squeaky, I thought), a tap-dance routine . . . and then a duet. Soon there were only two acts left.

I was watching the TV monitor when I suddenly felt someone pulling at my sleeve. It was Bonnie – and to my amazement she was white as a sheet.

"What's up?"

"I can't do it, Kate!"

"Can't do what?"

"I can't sing. Not in front of all these people!"

For the first time in all the years I'd known her, Bonnie had lost her confidence. She was actually shaking. I tried to encourage her – "you've got be brave in the music business!" – but it was no good.

"*You* sing for me," she said.

I stared at her in horror.

"No way," I said.

"*Please*, Kate! You're my best friend. And *somebody's* got to sing. I can't just drop out."

I felt like *I* was going to start shaking too. Get up, in front of all those people, all by myself – and sing? No band, no saxophone – just me? I hated the whole idea. But I could see that Bonnie was really upset. And I felt I was to blame. She *couldn't* sing that song. She sounded awful. I should have been strong enough to make her change her mind.

"Look," I said desperately, "I'll sing *with* you if you like."

That way we'd both get to look like idiots.

"No," Bonnie moaned. "I just can't!"

By now she was crying. One of her false eyelashes had come off and was perched on her cheek like a big hairy spider, while a load of eye make-up was running down her face.

"You'd do it for Jemima," she sniffed.

I hesitated.

"Yes, you sing, Kate," said a new voice. I blinked. Wild Thing was standing at my elbow. Before I could tell her to butt out, she went on: "You're a *good* singer."

I was so surprised I just goggled at her for a moment. "Do you really mean that?"

"You're *good*," said Wild Thing again. "Not like her," she added, pointing at Bonnie.

Then she went bounding off across the room after Hound Dog. I stared after her. I knew that Wild Thing wouldn't have said it if it wasn't true. I mean, she wouldn't say it just to make me feel better. Or to help Bonnie. No, she must really, truly think I was a good singer.

"*Please*, Kate," Bonnie moaned again.

I took a deep breath. "I can't believe I'm saying this but . . . OK."

They were already calling Bonnie's name. We ran to the stage door. I hissed, "Hey, Sam – lend me your guitar!" He looked surprised, but to my relief he didn't ask any questions. He just shrugged and handed me his guitar.

And suddenly there I was, in the middle of the stage, standing in front of a sea of faces. All of them looking at me.

Who was I kidding? *I* couldn't sing to all those people.

But I was going to have to. *You have to be brave in the music business*, I reminded myself. Then I checked that Sam's guitar was in tune.

I took a deep breath.

One thing that I *had* decided, in the split second before I went on stage, was that I wasn't going to sing Bonnie's song. It was too hard to sing without rehearsing – and besides, I didn't even know all the words. So what *could* I sing? And then I'd remembered the song I'd made up that first night at Gran's.

I said in a soft voice, "My name's Kate and I'm going to sing a song I've written called 'Homesick Blues'." I began.

"I got those homesick blues
I got those dog-gone blues
It's too long we've all been roaming
Yes, I got those homesick blues."

As I went on singing, this hush fell over the whole hall. It was absolutely quiet, except for my voice.

"There's an ocean lies between us
There's a whole plane ride between us
I just need it to be all four of us
I got those homesick blues.

I'm a-walkin' my dog – all alone
I'm watching my dog a-chewin' his bone
I'm just a girl who's missing her home-sweet-home
I got those homesick blues. . ."

But then something strange happened. I don't know why, because after that very first night at Gran's, I hadn't felt *that* bad. I'd sang the song a good few times since, in fact most times I'd practised my guitar, without feeling homesick the way I had that first evening. But now, as I stood on the stage, it all swept over me again. There really *was* an ocean between us and Dad, and that seemed an awfully long way.

The tears rose at the back of my eyes, and suddenly I was really, really scared that I was going to burst out sobbing in the middle of the talent show, in front of all those people.

I blinked hard. And it was at that moment that I suddenly spotted Gran out there in the audience. She was smiling at me. And . . . who was that next to her? I blinked again. It was Dad! MY DAD! He was home!

There was definitely a tear rolling off my cheek as I finished the song, but I didn't care. The audience was wonderful. They just exploded clapping. Some people were even cheering. And

Dad was waving at me and doing a thumbs-up.

I guess Wild Thing must be right. I CAN sing.

I came off stage in a bit of a daze. Bonnie hugged me. There were tears running down her face. "Oh, that was *so* beautiful," she howled. "The most beautiful thing I ever heard! They all love you. Oh Kate – why didn't *I* sing? Then everyone would love *me!*"

Typical Bonnie!

I shoved Big Sam's guitar at him and made for the door.

"What are you doing?" Bonnie demanded.

"I'm going to see Dad. He's out there in the audience."

"You can't! Not till they announce the winner."

"Oh." I'd forgotten all about that, to be honest. And I wasn't that interested, anyway. I just wanted to run out and give Dad a hug. But I supposed I'd better wait around.

The last act was really good – two break-dancers, and they put on a fantastic show, although I found it hard to concentrate. Then all the competitors surged out on to the stage so that the judges could announce the winner. Bonnie came too – even though she'd been too scared to perform!

I didn't really care who won. There had been so many good acts. I thought I might *even* be able to bear it if Wild Thing won! But still, you could have knocked me over with a feather when they read out the winner's name. Because. . .

IT WAS ME. I had won the Talent Show!

16

For the rest of that evening I felt like I was walking on air. It was one of the very best nights of my whole life.

The bestest bit of all was seeing Dad again. I hugged him and hugged him. He was really pleased to see us too, even when Wild Thing and Hound Dog came at him like a pair of cannonballs and took all the breath out of him. There were more hugs all round, and Gran even had a little weep, which I've never seen before, and when I asked her why, she said, "I'm just so proud of you all – well, not *Josephine*, of course, I've never been so embarrassed in my life!"

"She was funny, though," I pointed out. "Nobody could stop laughing." And Gran had to admit that this was true.

The next bestest bit was my prize – one hundred pounds, just for me, plus vouchers for the cinema and the ice-skating rink and bowling and lots of other things. I promised to take the whole band, including Bonnie, bowling the following week. Then we all said goodbye, and the band said *Congratulations* again, and they all hugged mc, even though they are boys. Bonnie gave me an extra special hug and said I would always be her Bestest Best Friend in the Whole Wide World!

So then we went home, stopping off for pizza on the way, and soon it was just Dad, Gran, Wild Thing and me, sitting around the table (and Hound Dog sitting underneath the table), gobbling down pizza.

I asked Dad how come he had flown home early.

He said, "The truth is, I really missed you all. And there was a few days' break in the schedule – a couple of gigs got postponed – and maybe it was daft – but somehow I just had to fly home."

"Does that mean you have to go back?" I asked. I couldn't stop my voice wobbling.

"Yes, I do have to go back, but – well, before I go into that, don't you want to see your presents?"

"Presents!" we yelled.

Dad had gone really mad on the presents. There were jackets and sweatshirts and baseball caps for me and Wild Thing, and a new skateboard for me, and chocolates, and Wild Thing had an enormous teddy with luminous orange fur. Gran had a bottle of her favourite liqueur, and earrings, and a sparkly T-shirt that said *New York, New York* and she was soon purring like a cat that's eaten all the cream.

"But that's not the best present," said Dad, grinning at us.

We gazed at him.

"I was thinking, girls – how'd *you* like to come to the States too?"

You can imagine what we thought! Though at first we just stared at him with our mouths wide open.

"Us come too?" said Wild Thing at last.

"To America?" I said. "In a plane, with you?"

"Well, I'm not suggesting we swim," Dad replied. Then he said we had school holidays next week, so why shouldn't Wild Thing and I fly out with him, and the three of us could all have a holiday. We wouldn't be able to take Hound Dog, but Gran said she would look after him for us.

"Of course," Dad winked at me, "after listening to Kate's song, I realize she might not want to go so far from her Home Sweet Home, but—"

"I do!" I screeched. "I do!"

And then we were all talking at once: the Big Apple . . . the Grand Canyon . . . Disneyland. . . Wild Thing got up and ran round the table on all fours, barking, and of course Hound Dog joined in. They knocked over a chair, and it fell to the floor with a crash. Luckily it didn't squash either of them. It's a wonder Mrs Crabbe didn't come to complain about the noise (or maybe she did, and we just didn't hear her).

I even gave Wild Thing a hug, I was so happy.
She gave me a lick on
the nose.

I didn't mind. She's a terror – but she's still
my sister. After all, if she hadn't told me I was
a good singer, I would never have dared go and
sing instead of Bonnie.

So, for once in my life, she had really done me a good turn.

I raised my glass. "A toast to Wild Thing!" I said. Then I looked down at Hound Dog, who was wagging his tail. "To the Wild *Things!*"

"The Wild Things!"

Dere Gran
  I et 8 donuts! Kate cuddent stop me!
  I luv yu!
  Josephine XXX

Dear Gran
  I helped Wild Thing write that email. I'm afraid it's true. She really did eat all those doughnuts. Greedy pig!
  Kate X
  PS They are yummy, I ate 3 and I had a malted milkshake too!

Dere Gran
  We hav a yello car.
  Its cool.
  Luv
  Josephine XXX

Dear Gran

It's a great car! It's the colour of a canary! And it means it's harder to lose, when you are parking in one of the giant parking lots here.

Kate X

Dere Gran
We went to the beche!
Josephine X

Dear Gran,

Wow – what a beach! Wonderful sand! Lovely warm sun. Dad said, "I'm going to watch Josephine like a hawk or she'll probably go and drown somebody," and then he went straight to sleep! We had to throw a bucket of water over him to wake him up.

Kate X

Dere Gran
  We went to Dizny!
  Josephine X

Dear Gran
  Today was probably the most embarrassing
day of my whole life. Wild Thing had a big
argument with Cinderella. She said she could tell
she wasn't real. She tried to pull off her hair.
Cinderella said she was going to call security!
Dad says he is never going to take us to
Disneyland again.
  Kate x

Dere Gran
  America is the best.
  Josephine XXX

  It is, Gran, but we miss you and we miss Hound
Dog. And we have great news. Do you know

what – Wes says we can all share him! He says Hound Dog is going to be our dog as well as his! I think even Dad is pleased, though he pretended he wasn't.

Wild Thing and me are THRILLED! Our own dog! He's part of the family now. And Wild Thing has promised she won't paint spots on him, and pretend he's a Dalmatian.

We're really looking forward to seeing you. Even though it means another ten hour transatlantic flight with Wild Thing – and Dad says the last one put years on him!

Lots and lots of love
Kate XXX

Dear Readers

Kate and Wild Thing have great fun looking after Hound Dog. But looking after a dog is a big responsibility and a lot of hard work. If you are thinking of getting a dog, make sure you have the time to take care of your pet properly. Dogs don't like to be left alone for long, and they need walking EVERY SINGLE DAY!

You also need to make sure your dog eats a healthy diet - not scraps from your leftover meals as some human food is poisonous to dogs, especially chocolate!

You can look at the following websites for more information on how to care for animals:

www.rspca.org.uk
www.scottishspca.org
www.pdsa.org.uk
www.sttiggywinkles.org.uk

Emma Barnes

Emma Barnes has always been a
bookworm. She was born and raised in Edinburgh,
where she spent hours making up stories for
her younger sister. Emma's first writing success
came when she won a short story competition –
the prize was a pair of shoes. Emma wears the
shoes for school visits, where she loves to spark
children's imaginations and create a passion for
writing and stories. Emma now lives in Yorkshire
with her husband, daughter and Rocky the dog.

www.emmabarnes.info